Praise for *¡Pa'que Tu Lo Sepas!*

"While cause-related anthologies aren't unusual, what clearly separates *Pa'Que Tu Lo Sepas* from the pack is the diligence and care the contributors obviously put into their work, and how deftly Angel Luis Colón curated the writers and their stories. This is an important, necessary, lovely collection, one that plunges the reader into the variety of cultures and beauty within the LatinX community. Truly, *Sepas* is magical, and filled with magical writing. A must-read, now and always."

—E.A. Aymar, author of *The Unrepentant*

PA'QUE TU LO SEPAS!

PA'QUE TU LO SEPAS!

STORIES TO BENEFIT THE PEOPLE OF PUERTO RICO

EDITED BY
ANGEL LUIS COLÓN

DOWN & OUT BOOKS

Down & Out Books
3959 Van Dyke Road, Suite 265
Lutz, FL 33558
DownAndOutBooks.com

Cover design by Zach McCain

ISBN: 1-64396-042-3
ISBN-13: 978-1-64396-042-5

Por mi gente

CONTENTS

BAD PUERTO RICAN
ANGEL LUIS COLÓN

Oh boy, here comes another charity anthology. I know, but I think this time we're writing for a damn good reason and one that's personal to me.

So personal, in fact, I didn't write a story.

An anthology for Puerto Rico, and I couldn't muster the nut to write a story, so here I am writing you a rambling foreword, and I don't have the faintest clue *what* being Puerto Rican is even about, I mean as a whole—it's not something simple in my eyes.

What the hell is a Puerto Rican? I'm not even sure I'm a good example of whatever it is people think of when they hear or see the words Puerto Rican.

Matter of fact, scratch that, I'm maybe even a terrible Puerto Rican.

It's not a statement of humility or a metaphor. I haven't visited the island in decades, the family I have there is estranged—that's putting it lightly—and I relate to other aspects of my cultural makeup more often than I ever find myself dancing down 5th Avenue on a hot June day.

I'm not sure where it started or ended. There's always

been a sense of pride, something deep inside me that knows who I am and why it is so very important. I like to think that immaturity kept that from me, but sometimes I wonder if it was shame—if I fell into the cultural trap laid out hundreds of years ago by the colonizers of a small island in the Caribbean. Over time, I've realized that no matter what, that island, that place, it still means everything. Without it, I'm just not me. Even if that me is a terrible Puerto Rican.

The story of those roots, they're not unique. Puerto Rico has always bent like the palm trees in the storm. Its history a maelstrom and its people still standing at the end of the chaos, perhaps changed, but always strong and firm on the ground. Since the day three terribly named Spanish ships arrived on its shores to bring disease, genocide, and loss to that island, Puerto Rico has always found itself picking up the pieces—beaten and bruised, but still with feet on the ground.

Isn't that the very story of Puerto Rico? Picking up the pieces and making something new, something entirely different, yet familiar and belligerently beautiful in its loudness? We pop against the sky: a blazing sunset of people promising an even more brilliant sunrise. Anger and laughter and passion incarnate: a people who know what it is to live on their terms.

My roots on that island are tenuous. Single generations born to European businessmen and criminals—people desperate to shed their identity and find a place on soil that was stripped away from its people not once but twice. Then these motherfuckers showed up, took wives, and had themselves babies. In a way, it was a third robbery.

Let's not even get into Project Bootstrap.

So anyway, I had Italian and Irish roots on that island. They disseminated, and a few families came from that. Within a generation, though, my grandparents all left. They moved to New York and made Nuyorican babies in the South Bronx projects. They built something new on ground that wasn't their own while those who immigrated before, who were there maybe even illegally, spat at them and tried to force them out.

Sounds familiar.

My grandfather: a man left to go to NYC on his own at nine years of age. Told to do his part. Worked at a printing press his whole life. He was the first Latinx in his union to run two presses at once. One of the first to demand a small bidding war when he chose to get paid the same as his white counterparts. He spoke terrible Spanish and loved Clint Eastwood movies. He dressed like Huggy Bear and spoke in a bizarre patois that my family still imitates today. He built himself up on his own terms.

My mother: divorced when I was three. A hairdresser by the time I went to kindergarten. She worked more than she mothered. She owned her own shop by the time I was twelve. She danced like a top and couldn't cook to save her life. She built herself up on her own terms.

But we build and build. Our genetic and cultural genocide? We found a way to dance to its rhythm—to rebuild what we lost into something entirely new. Our food, our laughter, our mixing of languages, of taking these things foisted upon us and making them entirely ours and nobody else's? This is our gift; this is what makes us a distinct light in a world so very full of darkness. We persevere. We take all that star stuff, all that tragedy, and all that diversity— los Tainos, los Borinquen, the African blood and European features—we build ourselves into something else. Maybe not quite what *belonged* on that soil, but something that stakes its claim and owns what it works for—we wear what we've made like goddamn gold.

And me? I'm a horrible dancer but a solid conga player. My Spanish isn't the best, but I can read or understand what's being said to me without issue. I have the timing fucking down on making an excellent pot of rice and can cook a mean mofongo if you need me to.

That's all the tip of the iceberg. Puerto Ricans are not alone in being this hodgepodge megaculture No, Spain made sure their reach was long, and we've got brothers and sisters and cousins in that big wide world out there that have had to build just as much as we have.

This project is also a bad Puerto Rican. It doesn't know what it wants to be, and it isn't even entirely Puerto Rican. This was a conscious decision. I wanted this slate of writers to feel the way I do about my identity. I wanted it to be everything and everyone while ultimately being something abstract—an idealized concept that lives ethereally because there is no finite definition to what we are. Honestly, if I were to cover the entire diaspora, it'd probably never be ready for publication (that would be a hell of a project, though).

These words, they are for Puerto Rico, specifically those who still suffer because Hurricane Maria and the racist infrastructure that demands the island of my ancestors be nothing more than a vacation hotspot that gets a little messy from time to time. That island will struggle and rebuild. They'll be hit again, whether by the storms or their hateful colonizers but still, they will stand up and make good from bad, new from detritus, and it will shine like the sun.

This is my way of giving back to a place I still don't know I belong but I sure as hell know has made me better for its presence in my life. It's a way of repping *all* my people—Puerto Rican, Mexican, Panamanian, Cuban, Ecuadorean, Dominican, Peruvian, and on and on. We're all in this shit together. We're stronger together. There's humor and pain in here. Not all crime like you were expecting and not all the protagonists are what you were expecting either. I wanted this to be varied and entirely against what anyone would expect—in my mind, the very essence of the island where so much of what I am came from.

It took a while to pull this together—false starts, the usual headaches of wrangling more than two writers into a project, and life itself—so it almost feels like we're late to this party. I mean, Maria was in 2017, right? Well, the island still needs help. It's why organizations like the Hispanic Federation are still looking for help and support to continue their efforts in Puerto Rico. There's a history of people forgetting the island and its troubles, so I don't think it would ever be too late to help.

Also, this is a hell of a collection—takes time to pull something this unique together.

I asked that these writers come in guns blazing. I wanted them unapologetically Latinx. I wanted them to get the word "spic" caught in the throat of every piece of human trash that's ever doubted us or hated us solely for our position in the long shitshow that is Western Imperialism. I wanted fiction that made people uncomfortable and made people remember their homes or abuelitas. No major themes or storylines, this book is a celebration of how utterly and beautifully different our cultures are, all of us screaming out for you to know exactly who we are and how we've built ourselves.

I can't think of anything more Puerto Rican than that.

I'll close with a few words from a favorite song—"Preciosa te llevo dentro. Muy dentro di mi corazón. Y mientras mas pasa el tiempo. En ti se vuelca mi amor."

This is for you, Puerto Rico, but maybe a little for me too.

To those of you reading—thank you.

Please buy books and read stories from other Latinx writers, especially the folks in this collection. Find stories and songs beyond your comfort zone and find knowledge, not just comfort, in words that may be alien to you.

THE BONES OF RIO RICO

DAVID BOWLES

February 2, 1928

Ah, how banal yet humbling to watch one's business fade. Despite my reputation as an imaginative merchandiser, despite my owning and operating the finest department store in the Rio Grande Valley, a decade of effort is slowly ebbing into nothing. Only eight years ago the local broadsheet praised the variety nestled within these walls: elegant little general store, high-fashioned specialty shop, millinery, and beauty salon. The best merchandise and bargains were always found here. Now the community's economic woes have forced me to close all but the dry goods and grocery departments.

Nonetheless, I ride here each morning from Alameda Ranch—the last of my profitable enterprises—and attend my sporadic customers. I suppose as I near my fiftieth decade on this earth, I simply crave human warmth. So many of those I loved have passed beyond—Father, Beatrice, my sweet Roberto. Though I feel great affection for my nephews and nieces, we have never been particularly close. And, of course, Mother's failing mind remembers less and less, so our conversations are one-sided at best. It seems, then, that fleeting contact with strangers and acquaintances must sustain me.

Today brought Hattie McLellan, sister-in-law of my late sibling Beatrice. Unaware of the recent attrition in my business, she had come hoping to have her hair styled in a bob, signaling to my mind the end of that fashion's novelty.

"I'm truly sorry," I told her. "But Daisy's still cutting hair out of her own front parlor. If you drop in, she'll be happy to oblige."

Hattie pulled at her curls with a bemused expression. "Yes, but that would mean driving into Weslaco. I'm not entirely sure I feel safe in that town, what with the rumors and all."

It was an invitation to gossip, so of course I played along. "And what, my dear, might those rumors be?"

"Haven't you heard, Miss Donna? Al Capone is here in south Texas. They say he wants to open a greyhound racing track just across the border. It seems he's residing in Weslaco and tipping big wherever he goes."

I shook my head in disbelief. "I guess I shouldn't be surprised, given the man who runs things on the Mexican side of the river."

Everyone knows Don Ernesto Arrendondo by reputation. The now Mexican town of Rio Rico, all 413 acres of it, used to sit north of the Rio Grande. But in 1906 the Rio Grande Land and Irrigation Company redirected the flow of the river without authorization, placing that tract of U.S. soil in a sort of international limbo. For the past twenty-two years, Arrendondo has reaped the benefits of this confusion, offering dog races, dance halls, cantinas, and entertainment not available in Texas, especially since Prohibition became the law of the land.

"With this new bridge being built between Weslaco and Río Rico, I'd bet the mob's curiosity is piqued," Hattie mused.

"Sure," I agreed. "And it's easy to imagine that Arrendondo might ally himself with Chicago crime syndicates."

She nodded. "Horrifying, isn't it, the thought of all that northern violence and vice piled atop our own local problems? More so with the disappearances."

"Of the children, you mean." This story I have been following closely. A child a month has gone missing from working-class Mexican families in the area. Officers of the law have done little to track down those responsible. Sheriff Baker swears his men are investigating, but I suspect this is mere hand-waving to ensure Mexican votes. The Texas Rangers, spread thin in order to quell violence in oil boomtowns, are abstaining from the case.

"Yes. Poor things," she declared before segueing into the ins and outs of her own family conflicts. I struggled not to berate her for such fleeting concern. Were the children Anglo, I'm certain both she and the authorities would make a much greater fuss. But we are products of our upbringing, are we not? I thank heaven that my childhood was spent under the care and guidance of "Auntie" Hester, whose compassion and Igbo sorcery are the keystones of my soul.

I closed the store early, the children weighing on my mind. After changing into trousers and a loose blouse, I went to stand amidst my alfalfa fields as the setting sun streamed pink-tinged gold upon my head. Brushing my fingers against the purple flowers of my unusually tall crop, I closed my eyes and sent my heart questing, using green magic to feel along soil and root. The droning of bees filled my ears as they swarmed about me, drawn by the gentle power.

I thrummed through the Green World, exploring the natural fabric that undergirds my community, grazing human spirits, attuned to the accustomed patterns, hoping to be jolted by any sense of wrong, any disturbance that might hint at the whereabouts of the missing boys and girls. Armed with this knowledge, I would go to the tenanches, let those old women take the necessary action. But the magic frayed at the very edges of my reach and once again I found no trace.

My heart heavy, I have retired to my humble home. I cannot help thinking of all the terrible things that might have befallen the little ones. Craving easy and dreamless sleep, I have drunk some chamomile tea infused with lime flower.

The dogs have leapt into bed with me. I pull them close and blow out the candle.

February 4, 1928

Though I swore seven years ago to get involved never-more in such potentially violent matters, I find myself drawn against my will toward a new maelstrom. I can only pray that this time I can rise to the task. Another failure, another death, will surely break me.

I had not quite left my home this morning when a tenta-tive knock stirred my dogs to a frenzy of barking. I shooed them aside and opened the door to find a young Mexican woman standing on my porch, flanked by three shy children.

"¿Señora Hooks?" she assayed in Spanish.

"Please, just call me Donna," I replied in the same language.

A little flustered by the intimacy, she hesitated before continuing. "My name is Isabel Quiñones, ma'am. I know I'm a stranger, but please believe that I come from a respectable family. My husband, Arturo, and I run a little fruit stand in Weslaco, down by the railroad tracks. We attend Mass each Sunday."

She seemed desperate for me to acknowledge her as a decent woman. Whatever she sought, it was difficult for her to come all this way and look me in the eye.

"Without a doubt, your standing in the community is blameless," I assured her, and she visibly relaxed.

"I'm terribly sorry to bother you at such an early hour, but I'm desperate for help. It's my son, you see. Jorge."

My stomach lurched with foresight. I lifted a hand as if to ward off her words, but she spoke, nonetheless.

"He's been taken, ma'am. Like the others."

Sighing, I stared past her at the sun, glowing white on a horizon swathed in winter fog. "I am not the right person, Mrs. Quiñones. You need to speak to the tenanches. They'll know what to do."

Her fingers plucked at the dark rosary around her neck. "You don't understand, Mrs. Hooks...Donna. The old women have already seen me. They told me to come to you. 'La güera santera,' they said. 'She will be your champion.'"

The Pale Witch. One of the many epithets I have collected down the years, most of them deserved. But I made it clear to the council after Roberto's death what my role would be in the welfare of this community, and it is frustrating that they have simply ignored my wishes in sending this poor woman my way.

Of course, I had no intention of dashing her hopes there on my doorstep. I would get her the help she needed, somehow. My heart ached to think of their suffering, their fear, their possible demise…

"Very well. Can you describe Jorge to me? Do you have something of his that you can lend me for a time?"

Handing me a wooden top and some marbles, she managed to give me details, her voice hitching constantly. Her oldest son is ten years old, nearly five feet tall, with striking hazel eyes and lanky black hair, a scar at the right corner of his mouth from a childhood accident. He was wearing black trousers and a blue shirt when he left his house yesterday morning. He never arrived at the schoolhouse for Friday classes. He never came home.

Of all the folk along the river's edge, I am the last woman who ought to make such promises, but her expression of anguish so moved me that I seized one of her hands and whispered with hoarse fierceness:

"We will get your son back, I swear."

Weeping, she kissed my cold fingers and swept her children off into the fog.

There was little point in going to confront the tenanches. They had decided to thrust this responsibility on me, so I would have to find an ally, a real champion for young Jorge Quiñones.

Getting in my Nash sedan, I headed south along rutted roads to the lushly wooded land on which Gabriela Rivera had established the retreat where she lived and practiced her shamanistic healing.

I found her in her garden, teaching an apprentice how to recognize and select herbs. Though approaching eighty years of age, Doña Gabriela seemed as sturdy as ever, barefoot among her luxurious plants, silver hair in a long braid that reached the hem of her orange skirt, a worn leather bag strapped across her immaculate white blouse.

Her impassive face was illuminated briefly by a smile as she crooked a rheumatoid finger at me.

"Come, Miss Donna," she called. "Anita here was just collecting ingredients for a poultice."

The younger woman curtsied and averted her eyes. My reputation, I suppose, preceded me.

"Ya métete. Ahorita voy," the shaman muttered, shooing her apprentice away. Turning back to me, she nodded. "So. A long time, no?"

"Yes, Doña Gabriela. And that's entirely my fault."

The shaman scoffed. "Course it is, silly woman. All caught up in making money. Bah. Whoever heard of a rich santera? Waste of your damn time."

I didn't disagree. Experience has taught me that arguing with Gabriela is pointless: she is stubborn as a mule and almost always right.

"I've come about the missing children," I explained, ignoring her long-standing criticisms of my lifestyle. "The tenanches sent a woman to me. Her son disappeared yesterday."

"And then? You already know how to track folk down. The hell you want from me?"

"It's not enough to find the children, Doña. They must be rescued."

The old woman reached out and grabbed her walking stick, which she had left leaning against a mesquite. She took a few hobbling steps toward me.

"Well, rescue them!"

I shook my head. "I can't. I need help. Don't you know someone? Some younger woman or man with enough power to confront the kidnappers?"

A look of dismay spread across her wizened face. "Whatever happened to that tough young witch I met twenty years ago, eh? Divorced, living alone in the monte, overseeing a passel of men workers with a shotgun in her hands? Trying to tell me you're afraid now?"

Grief squeezed my chest like a vice. "I'm not afraid of whoever or whatever has taken the children, Doña. I'm afraid of myself, don't you understand? I'm afraid of failing. Again. And the cost of that failure. People I love lost their lives because…because I wasn't adequate."

My eyes were blurred by tears, so I didn't realize the shaman had moved until I felt her warm, calloused palm on my face.

"Hush, Miss Donna," she whispered kindly, her breath smelling of eucalyptus and sage. "We ain't none of us 'adequate.' But the Virgin smiles down upon us with love all the same. Ain't no one can say if we will win or lose. Don't matter, in the end. What matters is we fought for order, for goodness, for innocence. We may suffer, but we suffer in the name of the Light, my daughter. You hear me?"

Her words loosened the knot in my heart. I laid my cheek atop her head, bending into her embrace. "I hear you, wise one. I have been selfish, not wanting to risk pain. But…very well. I accept the charge placed upon me. If the boy is still alive, I will be his champion. However, I will not seek revenge if he is dead. Others will have to enact justice."

Gabriela pulled away and nodded. "Fair enough, santera."

We conferred a while longer in that magical garden, speculating as to the identity of the child-snatchers and their possible weaknesses. Gabriela replenished my supply of rare but potent herbs, and I set out for my store.

It was well past 10 a.m. when I arrived. Several women were waiting impatiently on the sidewalk, unnerved by my tardiness on a normally lucrative Saturday. I attended them as quickly as I could, and then I drew up a sign to post in the window:

Closed until further notice—Management.

Now I am home. I have the afternoon to ready and equip myself. Tomorrow, come hell or high water, I will find young Jorge Quiñones.

February 5, 1928

It seems clear who is behind the disappearances. I will set out to confront them at first light. If I do not return, today's entry will be the last in my secret diary. Since anyone capable of reading it in my absence will perforce possess some degree of sorcery, I can only hope you will seek out and destroy the monsters responsible.

This morning, after I was certain the first Mass at Saint Joan of Arc had ended, I drove into Weslaco's "Mexican Town," just north of the railroad tracks. Frutería Quiñones stands close to that cultural dividing line, so I had no trouble locating it. A small but well-tended shack of wood and tin, the store boasts an entrance lovingly paved with rustic flagstones, and the family had set boxes of seasonal fruit just outside the door.

Isabel saw me first as I emerged from my car, and she hurried to me, beaming with expectation. I took great care to both curb her excitement and give her hope.

"Mrs. Quiñones, we have not yet found your son, but I have conferred with specialists, preparing myself. There are a few questions, however."

Somewhat crestfallen, she nodded and led me into the shack. Her husband was unpacking fruit from crates. Short but sturdy in build, Arturo Quiñones turned and regarded me with forced calm that belied the anguish I sensed within him.

"Good morning, sir. My name is…"

"I know who you are," he said gruffly. "My wife told me she approached you about our son."

"I must ask," I continued, ignoring his rudeness, "whether anyone has threatened you. Whether you have angered anyone. Especially…someone powerful."

Arturo swallowed heavily, but after a moment's hesitation, shook his head. "No, ma'am."

"Are you certain?" I prodded, convinced that he was not being honest.

At that moment, a woman thrust herself in our midst, hands clenched in anger. She was about Isabel's age, Mexican but light-skinned with green eyes. She wore a demure Sunday bonnet pinned to hair that had been drawn back into a severe bun at the nape of her neck. A high-collared, grey dress completed her church-going ensemble.

"He's lying to you," she said in English before looking pointedly at Quiñones and repeating for his benefit, "Le está mintiendo."

The fruit seller's eyes narrowed. "I warned you, Miss Leticia, to stay away from my family."

"I am trying to help, Mr. Quiñones! Even after you rudely rebuffed me at church this morning, I might add. I care very deeply for Jorge, and you need to tell the police the truth!"

Clearing my throat to catch her attention, I addressed the newcomer. "I'm sorry, Miss...Leticia, was it?"

"Yes, ma'am. Leticia Franco. I'm the schoolteacher at the Mexican elementary school. Jorge was one of my pupils."

"A pleasure. My name is Donna Hooks. I am...assisting the family in finding young Jorge."

Nodding, she glowered at the silent couple. "Well, that will be nearly impossible as long as they hide key information from you. Ask him, Mrs. Hooks. Ask him about the extortion."

It was my turn to glare at the man, but instead of putting the question to him, I turned to his wife. She knew what I was. "Tell me. Now."

Tears quivering in her eyes, she confessed. "It's Don Ernesto, from across the river. He demands protection money from us, sends his hoodlums to collect. Last year, the percentage increased. Many have refused to pay."

She shot a pregnant glance at her husband.

Leticia touched my arm. In a quiet but determined voice, she confirmed the suspicions welling within me.

"All the boys and girls who have gone missing are the children of merchants north of the tracks. Even more have been taken, but their parents paid the demanded ransom right away."

"And they were returned? What did they report?"

"They will not speak of what happened. I suspect they have suppressed some sort of trauma. Or perhaps fear has overwhelmed them. Arredondo refuses to return any child whose parents delayed in meeting his terms."

A sob escaped the lips of Arturo Quiñones. "Like I did! Oh, forgive me, God. I have failed my son!"

Leticia moved closer to him. "And still you will not talk to the police? Are you as frightened as the rest of the sheep who just turn their backs on their own children?"

I took hold of her arm and forcibly drew her into the sunlight. "That's enough," I said in English. "Let them be. They're terrified of what Arredondo will do to their other little ones if they denounce him to the authorities. Instead of railing indignantly, help me."

The schoolteacher arched a dubious eyebrow. "Help you? How?"

"Show me the path Jorge takes to school each day."

She scoffed. "To what end?"

"Someone or something took the boy. There may be clues to its identity."

"Ah, yes. You said you were assisting the family. Do you fancy yourself some sort of female gumshoe, Mrs. Hook? What can you possibly do that the police cannot?"

"Quite a bit," I snapped back. "I'm the Pale Witch, you see."

Her eyes wide, she crossed herself instinctively.

As we walked the few blocks to the shanty in which the Quiñones lived, Leticia shared her theories with me. A few weeks ago—visiting el pueblo americano on one of those Saturdays when Mexican women are patronizingly permitted to shop in the Anglo part of town—she had overheard socialite Deanna Board chatting with a friend. Mrs. Board claimed to have just sold her second house to a man named

Rhea, apparently a representative of Alphonse Capone.

Leticia was convinced that the Chicago gangster had been wooed by Don Ernesto. She had been distraught for weeks about the missing children, and the impending arrival of Capone acted as a catalyst, leading to her discovery of the links among the cases. From there, the conclusion seemed obvious. Such a criminal alliance meant a greater capital outlay, hence the hike in the cost of "protection" and the brutal extortion of those unwilling to pay.

"A fine piece of detecting," I offered. "Female gumshoe, indeed."

The schoolmarm smirked and gestured at an irrigation ditch running behind a row of meager homes. "Jorge walked along that canal to school from this brightly painted house. I'm not wearing the most appropriate shoes for such a hike, but I'm willing to accompany you."

We trudged up the clayey banks in silence, our eyes scanning the surroundings as we went. Eventually, the canal curved away, and I could make out the barn-like structure of the Mexican elementary school on a low rise just ahead. A well-worn footpath took us past a copse of mesquite, and there I found what I most dreaded.

Owl feathers. Large, black-fringed plumes, much longer than possible even for the biggest screeching predator on record.

"Oh, dear Lord," I breathed, kneeling to pick up one of the feathers.

"What is it? You look utterly mortified, Mrs. Hooks!"

I stood, running my finger along the vanes, wincing at the dark energies they contained.

"Lechuzas," I managed to say at last. "Witch owls."

* * *

After leaving the teacher at her school, I made my way back to my car. I would have to make one more visit, I knew, before honing in on Jorge Quiñones. If, as it appeared, shape-shifting witches were assuming the form of giant barn owls and snatching children away, I required the most current information on the parliament's numbers and its possible location.

That meant going to La Hierbería Guadalupana and facing Roberto's mother, a woman who rightly despises me, blaming me for the death of her only son.

My chest aching at the thought of the encounter, I nonetheless stood by my promise. I am the boy's champion. I will face what I must.

I entered the cool gloom of Doña Élida's store. She was hanging ristras of garlic and turned her head slightly to look at the entrance. Grunting, she made her laborious way back down her step ladder and stood to face me, her steel-gray hair clamped down by a net. Behind her, candles flickered weirdly near the dark passage into the less wholesome area of her apothecary. Since Roberto's death, Élida Ramírez has irrevocably changed. She will sell anything to anyone, even the darker sorcerers of these parts.

Squat and toad-like in her black shift, she seemed the very antithesis of Doña Gabriela.

"I told you to stay away," she said after a moment.

"Yes, and I would not bother you were it not important."

Her rheumy eyes narrowed. "Speak, then."

Pulling the feather from my bag, I thrust it at her. "The missing children. A witch owl took at least one of them. I need to know if there is a parliament of witches nearby."

Doña Élida coughed wetly, drawing a handkerchief from somewhere on her person and spitting into it with a grimace. "And what will you do with such information, gringa maldita?"

Cursed white woman. My cheeks were burning, but I choked back tears and harsh words. "The tenanches have chosen me to rescue a boy."

Her laughter was low and horrible, a mirthless moan. "Rescue a boy. Like you rescued my Roberto, you pallid bitch? The tenanches are more senile than I had imagined."

Stoic, I returned her burning gaze. "I won't bother apologizing again. But Roberto's loss nearly destroyed me as well, you know."

"Would that it had," she growled. "You have no business interfering with powerful men and women armed only with that weak African magic you learned at your nurse's knee, not even adding the piddling potions and spells you got from Gabriela."

I waited, seething with grief. After a moment, she jerked the feather from my hands.

"Yes. There is a coven nearby, in Río Rico. A group of young witches hired by Arredondo to safeguard his operations. Between the thirteen of them and the hard men they work with, they are going to rip you apart. Go now, Hooks. Go and be damned."

So now I lie in the darkling upon my bed. My equipment sits waiting for dawn. I think of my encounter with the Luminous seven years ago, how those blood-sucking sorcerers batted my magic aside, laughing. I remember Roberto, calloused hands clutching the air as his life was drained away, my limbs locked by a spell I could not counter. But it is time to set aside the failures of the past. Tomorrow I either prove myself worthy of the old women's trust, or I join my beloved there Beyond.

February 6, 1928

Allies arise where one least expects them, even on the very plains of Hell.

I drove to the river this morning and took the ferry across. In the foggy twilight, the pilot mistook me for a man, all decked out as I was in boots, trousers, mackintosh, and slouch hat, a shotgun in the crook of my arm. I did not bother to correct him. To the east loomed the pylons of the nascent bridge, like the bones of some antediluvian dragon.

On the far bank, I stood among the reeds. Clutching Jorge's toys in my free hand, I sent my green magic threading outward, feeling for the soul whose essence lingered on his prized possessions. Without warning, my senses slammed into a vast area of wrong, of sick, of evil. Staggered by the intensity of the magical recoil, I dropped to one knee in the mud.

In the midst of that malignity, Jorge Quiñones trembled, still alive against all hope.

I stowed the toys in my pocket and broke into a run, pulling chi from the Green World around me to sustain my middle-aged flesh. About a mile from the river, a mansion sat among a pecan grove, a fleet of black Model A sedans flanking its ample verandah. Arredondo's home. Giving it a wide berth, I slowed, the cold touch of evil a nauseous wave.

Behind the mansion loomed a wooden barn, weathered and ominous. Beyond it, a field of bones stretched away south.

Human bones. Children's bones. Dozens. Hundreds. The Green World squirmed with their restless souls, trapped by vicious and murderous and lonely deaths. Oh, how they clutched at me! Oh, how they cried for release! But I steeled myself, ignored their pleas. My first duty was to the living.

Shuddering, I lifted the shotgun and rounded the barn until, standing in the midst of all that wreckage, that death, those plaintive lost souls, I faced the open door.

"Jorge!" I called. "Jorge Quiñones!"

With a startled sob, a boy-shaped silhouette appeared in the entrance.

"That's it, son. It's okay. Your parents sent me to get you. Just come on out of there. Come to me."

Jorge assayed a few cautious steps. His clothes were in tatters, smeared with blood. His eyes were wide with fear and hope.

"My parents?" he asked, emerging fully into the slanting light of dawn.

And then the witch burst from the barn—an enormous screech owl with lifeless black eyes, a vicious curving beak and talon-tipped wings that gripped the shoulders of the terrified child before he could take another step.

"Step back!" it shrieked in a harrowing voice. "Step back or I claw out his throat!"

Training the shotgun on the shifted witch, I complied, searching for an opening.

"All I want is the boy!" I called. "Turn him over, and I will leave in peace."

The monstrosity cackled madly. "You stupid bitch! My sisters are already on their way! We felt you coming! There will be no peace!"

Someone came running from the house, but it was not another witch. I spared a glimpse at the hefty young man in the expensive suit as he pulled up short, regarding the human-sized owl with incredulity—I had seen his scarred face in enough newspapers to recognize him as the infamous Alphonse Capone.

Behind him, there did come a black-clad witch in human form, along with an elegant fellow I assumed was Ernesto Arredondo. They were flanked by men with tommy guns, both from Río Rico and Chicago judging by their appearance.

"What in the hell?" Capone began, just as a tall, young Mexican criminal raised his machine gun.

His bullets would wound or kill the boy. Instinctively, I thrust my left hand into the air, sketching a glyph that wrenched the weapon from the mobster's hands.

On the edge of my perception, I felt the witches gathering, drawing closer. They would all converge at once, I knew. Too many. Too powerful. I would be overwhelmed. Despair edged into my mind. I was going to fail, again. People were going to die.

Then I took another sidelong glance at the newcomers, their weapons. A glimmer of hope. The ghost of a plan.

"You men, stop right there," I said. "I'm here for the boy. And to stop this coven from ever hurting another child."

Capone ran his hand down his face, trying to regain his composure. "Coven? Who are you?"

As if in answer, the witch beside him stepped forward as her sisters emerged from the morning mist. Now there were twelve in a ring around the field of bones. "It's her," one of them hissed. "La pinche güera santera."

Ignoring them, I turned my head slightly. "You're Capone, aren't you? I heard a rumor you were staying in Weslaco. Let me put it this way: I don't interfere with the crimes of men. If you and this other gentleman want to smuggle alcohol across the border, that's none of my concern. But your partner has been employing shape-shifting witches, lechuzas, to collect protection money from business owners in Weslaco. When they don't pay, the creatures kidnap a child for extortion. If the money isn't ready soon enough, these witch owls kill the child."

Keeping the shotgun steady, I sent green magic down into the corrupt field. Listen, I whispered to the children's squirming souls. Listen. Let me show you the way. They clung to my power with eager hope.

"What?" Capone turned to Arredondo. "Is this true, you son of a bitch?"

I guided the spirits, twined them with the stunted roots that lay beneath their bones.

Arredondo shrugged and said nothing.

"Believe me, Mr. Capone. This boy's mother came to me yesterday, begging for help. I'm here to end this atrocity. You can either side with them and be damned, or you can help me."

"This broad," Capone muttered, turning back to me. "Help you how?"

Now. Now, children.

"Kill them. Kill them all."

The earth burst open at the foot of each witch, green tendrils of spirit and plant winding around their legs as they struggled and screamed.

Capone appeared to quickly appraise the situation. Don Ernesto had fled. The young criminal I had disarmed was trying to unjam the weapon he had retrieved. And the women in black were transforming. Their clothing morphed into feathers, their faces twisted into beaks, their arms widened into vast, cruel wings.

Facing his men, Scarface shouted. "Fill those goddamn monsters with lead, boys!"

His team fired upon the witch owls. The one holding Jorge pulled its beak and talons just far enough away from the boy's throat—I squeezed the trigger, wending magic around the pellets to keep them from scattering. The lechuza's head exploded in a profusion of gore, and I rushed to Jorge's side, wrapping my arms around him.

Several of the fiends, though wounded, broke free of the tendrils and hurled themselves into the air. They plunged toward the boy and me, wailing and gibbering.

"Amen!" I shouted, lifting a hand and twisting my fingers in a ward. "Aeternam vitam! Resurrectionem carnis!"

The Latin words, an inversion of the Apostles' Creed, repelled them for a moment, but the witch owls screeched in fury and redoubled their attack. Capone snatched the tommy gun away from the young Mexican mobster and took aim, unleashing a barrage of bullets against the winged monsters above my head. In moments, the bodies of the women sprawled lifeless among the bones.

I pulled Jorge away from my embrace and began to look him over. His eyes flitted over the dead witches, spilling tears of relief when he realized his ordeal was over.

"Are you okay?" I asked. "Were you seriously wounded?"

He shook his head and stood a little taller, wiping his nose on a tattered sleeve. Sustained by a stiff pride that reminded me of his parents, he spoke in a hoarse whisper.

"They were going to eat me. That's what they said. Eat me while I watched."

Hollow eyes. Shell shock. Pulling the top and marbles from my pocket, I placed them in his hand.

"Come on. Let's get you home." I took his hand and began to lead him away, using my boots gingerly to move aside the bones. They were silent and still now.

To my right, Capone's men hurried to his side, checking to see whether he'd been wounded.

At his gesture, they seized the young Mexican who had remained though Don Ernesto had fled. They forced him to his knees. Scarface spat on the ground.

"What was your name again, gunsel?"

"Me llamo Juan Nepomuceno Guerra Cárdenas."

"All right, Johnny. You find your boss," Capone said, "and you take him out. In a few years, I'll come looking for you. You got a good operation going; maybe you and me can do business. But no black magic or witches, capisce? And no goddamn kids, fer chrissakes."

He tossed the machine gun at the youth and approached us. I kept walking.

"Lady," he said, "I don't know who you are, but you are one gutsy dame."

I smiled despite myself. "Thank you, I guess."

"Do you need anything? A ride? Money?"

Pulling Jorge closer, I stopped and turned to regard Capone.

"Just one thing, please."

He doffed his hat in an awkward gesture of respect. "Name it."

"Burn the witches and bury these bones."

Scarface gave a sober nod and put his men to work.

As black smoke filled the morning air behind me, I guided the boy north, toward hearth and home and happy embraces for us both.

At last, a victory. Life has taught me that such joy is fleeting, that darkness will creep back into the world and challenge me afresh. But for now, the dead are still, and my heart is light. I have left my fear and grief upon that field of bones, fading into the Green World like the souls of stolen children.

BOBBY'S LEAVE—1968
DÉSIRÉE ZAMORANO

Years later, the first miscarriage was what Manuel remembered the most vividly. The horror, the shock of the life cut off abruptly, the pain that wracked his wife's body, the missing new life.

While Lita recovered at their City Terrace home, her brothers Bobby and Roland visited and collided with each other in the doorways of their tiny apartment astonishingly making Lita laugh, full-throated, and told her their stories and misadventures of their farm up in Goleta that each year barely scraped by.

And her brothers were grown up, long, and loping and sangre de leche, as Lita said, slow to work, slow to rise, but quick for visits that included meals.

"That's fine by me," Lita said, directing their simmering of the chile verde, later watching Bobby dish it out alongside the rice and beans Roland had made along with mounds of corn tortillas.

Roland, the oldest, the tallest, the laziest, was drafted first, but he was rejected, he told them, with a long, slow smile. "What can I say? Born under a lucky star, I guess."

"If that were true, you wouldn't have been born Mexican," his brother Bobby prodded at him.

Two miscarriages. Before Lita's third pregnancy, she and Manuel had moved from their apartment to a home in Mount Washington.

Lita wanted to work, and she wanted to have babies. She worked slowly, diligently at her nursing degree, but by her third pregnancy, her doctor, a gruff man with a bristly white mustache, demanded complete bed rest. "Don't even think about moving," he glowered.

Despite his sense of concern and anxiety, Manuel enjoyed the sense of waiting on his wife. This was something he could do. The baby bedroom was now a pregnancy room. In the morning, he brought her coffee and conchas, made her a sandwich for later, kissed her belly, kissed her, and went off to work. He did not want her to see the worry and fear in his face and his body. They hired a young girl from down the street who would check in on her in the afternoons, bring her water, help her to the bathroom.

Lita lost the baby at five and a half months.

As their baby, their son, died, the hospital staff wouldn't let Manuel near her. When she returned home, he hadn't any desire to buy flowers. He couldn't pretend there was any joy, and neither could she.

"I want to sleep in our room tonight," she said.

His chest filled with love and warmth and gladness that they could hold each other, chastely, that they could rescue each other.

"Alone," she said.

That first night was filled with thoughts of inadequacy and failure that rippled over him, again and again. Manuel had lost her. How would he live without her? He quietly wept for the babies, for Lita, and for himself.

Lita didn't speak to Manuel. He knew it was more that she was unable to speak to him. How could he be so lost without her, when it was clear he needed to find their way? He had no words that soothed or consoled her. She soothed and cared for and softened him. How could he not do the same for her?

This time there were no visits filled with laughter. Bobby was in training at Ft. Ord. Roland ducked in and out, sitting in her room while Manuel worked, then headed back home the next day to Goleta.

After Roland left, he came again with coffee and conchas and a kiss on her head, and she responded with, "Please go away. Please go to your job."

He did. He was a burro again. He returned that evening, and the house was quiet, as if it were empty. Terror gripped his chest. Had she abandoned her misery here and him along with it? Had she returned to her family in Goleta?

She lay in their bed, asleep, the coffee and sweet bread untouched.

He sat at the kitchen table. He sat and waited. When it was nine o'clock and she still slept, he pulled out the lunch meat, made himself a sandwich, ate it, then went to sleep in what had been her pregnancy room.

Was it a week like that, or a month? When it came to misery, it was hard for Manuel to keep track; misery bled into the days and nights, into the smile of strangers and praise of his supervisor. If Lita was at the bottom of an unlighted cave, unsure of how to escape, his heart was there with her, without an exit pass, without a treasure map, without a guide.

What was he supposed to do?

He went to work.

Sometimes he would return early, and her bedroom door was closed. She was already asleep, a book splayed on the bedspread, the light on, her full lips lightly parted.

He wanted to kiss those lips.

Or he could find someone else. He shook his head against the thought. It was Lita he wanted, Lita the young girl he married, the brown and smiling, teasing, mocking woman who had once loved him. He wanted her eyes on him, her mouth on him, her love in his direction.

As the months passed, she went back to school, and Manuel continued to work. Manuel dreamed of touching Lita again. Dreamed of being with her again, dreamed of the warmth and softness returning, dreamed of being a man and wife again.

It was if they were both doing penance for a crime, a sin, neither of them had committed.

Bobby showed up, on leave for a few days, slick and clean and gleaming. His time in training had filled out his frame with lean muscle, carved down the fat, burnished his skin tone. Set against his dark face, his eyes and teeth gleamed, particularly when he smiled, as he did now, like he had found his place in the world and owned it.

That was, Manuel thought, because of Alice. Alice sat on Bobby's lap, and Bobby's arms were always around her, around her waist or her shoulders or her legs in short shorts like he owned them.

It tugged at him, like baby buggies and baby clothing tugged at Lita. What the two of them had both lost.

For now, Manuel argued. For now, not for all time.

The four of them sat on the back patio that Manuel had begun to reshape and mold into his vision.

Bobby leaped up, brushing Alice off his lap, and followed Lita back inside the home.

Alice sat there, her plump, freckled pale thighs jiggling as she nervously tapped her leg. "I think your home is the most amazing place. It's like a castle up here, you know?" She smiled a shy smile, showing upper teeth that crossed over each other.

"I forget where you two met," Manuel said.

"Dancing! He was looking so fine in that uniform, and so brown and manly, you know?" She wriggled her shoulders as if laughing at herself.

"He came up to me and asked me to dance, and I told him I didn't know any zoot suit moves, and he laughed, telling me that was like a lifetime ago and good thing too, cuz neither did he. God made Mexicans so beautiful, you know?"

The way she said that caught Manuel off guard.

She moved right next to him, conspiratorially, and now Manuel was overconscious of the dimple in her thigh and the cleavage exposed by her halter top. Her chest was rosy pink, like her cheeks, either from too much sun or a little nervousness.

"I don't know if Bobby's gonna tell you. You know he seems such an open kinda guy, which is why I think he's so swell, but the truth is..." she looked around nervously, stopped by having heard the back-door swing, but it was a neighbor's back door. "We're gonna have to get married, if you know what I mean. You're a married man, a man of the world. He wants to make it a civil service, and my old man passed last year, my mother's in Fresno and has already yelled at me for even stepping out with a Mexican, so do you think you could stand with us at the court this week? You and Lita are so sweet, and you know, you're so grown up compared with us."

Manuel looked into those nineteen-year-old eyes, blue, under the stiffly arched and painted brown eyebrows.

"As long as it's good by Lita, it's good by me."

"Bobby's probably asking her right now. I wanted to ask you. That's what I love about you two. Bobby says it's always about the other one; it's never about yourselves, you know? How do you do that?"

"Stop giving my cuñado an eyeful!" Bobby said, yanking Alice by the arm, pulling her away from Manuel.

Is that what she was doing? Is that what he was doing? Manuel blinked at himself, trying to scrabble out of this uncomfortable position when Lita came in.

"I feel a little embarrassed," she said, looking at Alice. "I wish I had something more festive to offer the two of you, but," Lita raised her glass, "to the love between you, and to the young life you two have started together."

They joined her in raising and clinking their glasses, then sipping.

That night, Lita knocked at the door of where Manuel now slept.

"Come back to me," she said. "Come hold me."

That was what he wanted; of course, he wanted more, but he wanted to hold that warm body close to him, feel the rise and fall of her breathing, listen to the soft purr of her voice. He wanted the nineteen-year-old Lita back to him—not her body, not the bones, but the brightness of her eyes and her laughter. Now holding her next to him, he could offer himself a little hope that that part of Lita would return.

"I'd forgotten how good you smell," he said, his arms

wrapped around her waist, her back to him. His body was coming immediately to attention, and he was trying to quell it, because he knew, he knew, that was not the reason his wife had invited him back into their bed.

She shook her head.

He squirmed, "Ignore it. Ignore me. I just want to hold you."

She stared up at the ceiling. She sighed. "I don't know if I can explain it to you, Manolo."

"Try me, try." Please, don't ever kick me out of the bedroom. Please, let me stay here, in bed with you, forever. Please, let me be.

"Every time, every time, every damn time I see someone, I can't help but think, 'They used to be a baby. Some stupidly lucky woman gave birth to them.' I can't help it. Every time I see anybody, all I can think is some stranger, some woman, could do—without even thinking—what I've been aching to do, for you. For us."

Manuel listened, inhaled her scent, and stroked her arm. He had almost forgotten how soft her skin was, how smooth, how warm. He had gotten his body under control—if he listened to her words and paid no attention to how sweetly the two of them fit together—

"And then that little girl, that little *girl*, is going to have Bobby's baby. She's going to make us an aunt and uncle before I can make us parents. I just don't understand." She wriggled free from him and turned to face him.

"How can I live with this pain, Manuel? Every single day. It just hurts too much."

He picked up her hand and kissed the tips of her fingers. "We haven't even started. I mean, we could go to doctors, see what's wrong with me, see how to fix it—"

She pulled her hand away. "See what's wrong with *me*, you mean." She shook her head. "I had a mother who put three people in this world. I asked my dad if she ever had problems, and he shook his head and told me those weren't things they talked about. Maybe she had problems too."

"Maybe," Manuel grasped at the change in her mood. "Maybe we will get through this, and then you can have your three babies."

She turned to lie on her back and gaze up at the ceiling. He watched her breasts move with her breathing. She said, "Maybe that is how things will work out." Then she turned to him mischievously, "I thought you wanted four!"

"You want four. I want what you want."

She lay back down with a heavy sigh.

"It's just, part of life, like breathing. Do I *want* to breathe? I don't even think about it. But not being able to have a baby, it becomes the only thing I think about. Do you understand?"

He said, "A little." But no. Not really. Lita's thoughts had a wider range than his own.

"I'm glad, even if it's just a little," she said. "Everything, everything is a sign of God's handiwork, you know?"

"Maybe God's handiwork wasn't ready," he said.

Pulling him toward her, she said, "I've missed you."

Manuel held her close to him, inhaling her scent, feeling the tug and pull of her body, both falling toward the other.

That night, she held him as a woman holds a man.

Friday, Lita pursed her lips at City Hall as she eyed Alice's belly, but took the pictures.

Alice, in a baby blue dress with a lace-fringed scoop neck, clung to Bobby, grabbing his arm, following wherever he led. Bobby, swaggered in his dress uniform, talked to

Manny, Roland, and Lita almost as if Alice weren't there, described his plans for after the Army, where he'd like to live, how he hoped to be a mechanic when he returned, how he hoped he'd be getting a lot of experience doing that where he was stationed.

They hopped in a red car and headed to Olvera Street.

"We don't have anything like this back in Fresno," Alice exclaimed.

After putting a second roll of film in her camera, Lita stopped a stranger to take their picture in front of the bandstand on the plaza. Bobby insisted on taking them to drinks and dinner at one of the fancier restaurants, where Bobby drank 7 and 7s and ordered a bottle of Mateus Rosé for the table while Roland and Lita drank a Coke. Bobby asked the mariachi band to serenade his new wife. Roland fought with Manuel over who paid the check, and the loser, Roland, tipped the trio.

After the songs were sung, the meal eaten, the drinks drunk, and conversation lulled, Bobby emptied his glass, looked at his watch, then at Alice and said, "We should go." He ran his hand over Alice's thigh; she looked at him expectantly, smiling the way she had done all day. "I need to spend my last few hours of leave with Alice."

Manuel tapped Bobby on the shoulder and said, "Keep your head down, you hear? Come back for your beautiful new wife."

"I got that covered," Bobby said, grinning like the world was his.

Lita came up to him and hugged him tightly. "Come home. Just come home."

They watched Bobby and Alice trail through the street, heading toward Union Station while Roland loped toward the Greyhound bus station.

Manuel and Lita held hands and walked slowly the other way. Lita stopped at the fountain, dug into her bag, and stood there, dropping penny after penny into the water.

Years later, Manuel came across the photograph of the five of them: Roland, smirking, towering above the group; Lita, smiling broadly, bright red lipstick against the sheen of her brown skin and dark hair, a green halter top that emphasized the lift of her breasts and made him long for her even more than usual. Alice muffed it, her eyes closed, a goofy grin revealing the two tangled front teeth. Bobby's hand proprietarily around her waist, provocatively close to her breast, and Manuel, a small, strained smile.

So many things had happened after Bobby's civil ceremony that they didn't get around to developing the film until five months after the wedding picture had been taken, three months after Bobby's death had been officially announced, and two months after his funeral at their church in Goleta.

Lita's next pregnancy held.

Alice didn't attend the funeral; in fact, they never saw her again.

ME ENCANTA TU NOMBRE

Carmen Jaramillo

Jack Steiner-Casillas reclined in front of the open balcony doors with his eyes almost closed, letting the light from the sunset rest on his arms. His cousin and sister sipped wine and beer behind him at the kitchen counter.

"...so, the long and short of it is, the agency that's basically Panamá's EPA has always been more concerned with using environmental resources for tourism and development rather than, y'know, sensible long-term conservation."

His cousin Freddie rested one hand on her hip and the other on the counter, next to her glass. His sister Lola sat on a barstool facing their older cousin.

"So that's what caused the shortages you were talking about in um...in Herrera?"

All of the Casillas cousins were born in the United States, but Freddie had moved back to Panamá with her father almost nine years before.

"More or less, that's droughts made worse from bad management and waste. There's water there, but you've got all this tourism business straining the resources. It's all fragile. And it'll get worse over the next decade. So that's what these new laws are about, it's *real* long-term management. It's the strongest water protection legislation Panamá has ever had."

Jack shut his eyes, focusing on the sounds from a little open-air bar down at street level, hoping the music and laughter of the locals would drown out their political yakking.

"...whole thing would be falling apart if it wasn't for Navarro."

That politician's name had already butted into his day, somehow. Maybe he'd read it from the car that afternoon, on the garish billboard sticking out over the causeway where it joined the mainland. They'd been driving back from the boardwalks and cafes along the cluster of little islands, where Freddie said the American military base used to be, and he'd tipped his head to gaze around the billboard and at the chain of palm trees on the shoreline leading to the city.

"...representatives for all the farmers, the indigenous comarcas, construction firms, and the hotels—and of course those companies are mostly all based here in the city. It's a very delicate agreement."

Jack stretched his neck closer to the balcony, almost believing he could smell the salt from the Pacific Ocean in the distance.

Freddie's voice paused, and Lola snickered.

"Hey. Jacky's falling asleep."

Jack sighed and leaned over one armrest, turning his head to face the girls.

"I only get to come to Panamá once a year, sometimes

not even that. I don't wanna waste my visit talking about political shit."

Lola made a face at him. For the party Freddie would bring them to, Lola had conditioned and styled her hair like their cousin's and wore a borrowed dress.

"Political shit…Jesus, d'you even *know* what we're talking about?"

"Some politician who's all fancy and popular."

Freddie was grinning at him. His cousin had invitations to parties, weddings, and quinceañeras every weekend, where she shared champagne with half of Panamá City.

"Just no interest at all, huh?"

"He never has *any* interest in what's going on here or what anything actually is. It's why he's always so clueless when we're here."

He popped out of the chair.

"The fuck? I'm not clueless!"

"Aw, Jacky, don't get mad."

Freddie stepped forward and patted his cheek, but Jack twitched his head away.

"I'm not *mad*, you're just wrong."

"Well, we were just talking about the party a minute ago, you don't seem to have too much interest in it."

"Yes, I do, I've been waiting for it."

"You're not gonna be able to talk to many people if you don't know any Spanish, though…"

"I *do* know Spanish!"

She leaned into her hip, her thin gold bracelets jingling when she folded her arms.

"Okey. Me 'tas jodiendo, awebao?"

Jack froze and focused, running each word through his memory. He felt heat on the back of his neck as he began to nod.

"Yeah, yeah. Exactly."

Freddie's grin widened across her teeth.

"Dude..."

Jack twisted his head to face his sister.

"She asked if you were bullshitting her."

The girls cackled. Jack flushed. He grabbed his beer glass from the table and swept out onto the balcony.

Jack leaned against a wall a few feet from the bar table and watched the guests in cocktail dresses and silk shirts float through the hallways and living rooms with easy smiles. Some were in their early twenties like him, and others were old enough to have grown grandchildren. Freddie moved between groups, catching up with everyone she knew. She'd sidle up to her cousins from time to time to point out a bank president, the owner of Panamá's biggest car dealership, or their kids. Lola looked stiff and a little unsure, never blending in. And Jack never noticed her speaking Spanish.

He sipped Cardenal Orgaz Panamanian rum with Coke, even though prosecco was on offer. Freddie had introduced him to a few other English-speaking guests, but he couldn't shake off a self-consciousness he wasn't used to. He never had any trouble at parties back at college in Minneapolis, where he flashed his heritage like a pair of red Air Yeezys. His was a rare name in a sea of Ryan Petersens and Brendan Larsons; the girls cooed over it. He told them where Panamá was, and they dreamt up visions of lush trees and hot, humid beaches. But now, actually standing in Panamá, he drank by himself.

"You interested in something, Jacky?"

He blinked; Freddie had appeared next to him.

"What d'you mean?"

She glanced over at a little group of people.

"You've been gawking at that woman in the purple dress over there."

He'd noticed the long-legged woman in a deep violet wrap dress from time to time, unable to hear her voice but seeing the warmth in her smile as she greeted the other guests who approached her with bright, animated faces. Jack could never watch her for long; she kept moving through the room, never staying in one conversation.

He sniffed at his cousin.

"I'm not gawking. And yeah, maybe I am interested."

"You don't mind she's literally twice your age?"

"What?"

"She's at least forty, probably more."

"I say thirty-five."

"Bullshit, I promise she's over forty."

"Whatever, she's a *good* forty."

Another man had approached the woman. She held her neck straight and shoulders back, as if ropes of diamonds were draped over her chest.

"You know who she is?"

Jack refused to look at his cousin's grinning, smarmy face.

"No. So what?"

She just chuckled again, patting Jack on the shoulder as she walked away.

"Nothing, no reason. Good luck with her..."

He brushed her off. The woman in the violet dress began to pull away from the man; with a gracious nod and hand motion, she stepped back through the groups of people and moved out of sight down the hallway.

She'd slipped away from two other men that way during the evening. Jack pictured himself sauntering over to her and offering to refill her drink, like he would any night. But tonight, he couldn't stop himself from seeing her giving him a polite refusal and walking away.

He fidgeted, digging his thumbnail into the ridges of his glass. Freddie's joke from before the party still nagged at him. He really did feel proud when he looked up at the moon, so massive this close to the equator, and saw it lighting up the silvery waves in the bay. Or when he saw the forest-covered Cerro Ancon, the hill towering over the city's western edge, with its colossal Panamanian flag at the summit. The moment he stepped off the plane onto the jetway every trip and took his first gulp of hot, wet air, he swore he felt his lungs shiver. Like his Panamanian blood still recognized the air it came from.

Through the pair of wide glass doors out to the patio, he stared at the condo towers on the next block, lit up in green and gold. Before leaving town, he'd even bragged about this party to his friends. What was wrong with him? He tried to find the right word for how he felt. He winced; no, not clueless.

"Would you mind refilling my glass?"

Jack snapped his head up. The woman in the violet dress stood in front of him, staring him in his eyes. She held up an empty champagne flute.

"Oh...sure. Of course."

He stood close to the bar table, but the woman could easily have slid around him to help herself. With a careful hand, he took the woman's flute and began to pour prosecco. She motioned to Jack's glass, where he'd set it down on the bar, after taking back her own.

"You should pour some for yourself too. All the ice in your drink has already melted."

"Yeah, yeah, good idea."

He pushed the rum aside to fill a new glass of his own. She held up hers for a toast.

"Salud."

They drank. The woman spoke with an accent, but her English was perfect. She kept watching him, her eyes fixed on his face, as she lowered the glass.

"I don't think we've met yet."

"We haven't, no. I'm Jack Steiner-Casillas. If you know Freddie Casillas, I'm her cousin."

She sipped more prosecco. Her eyes glittered.

"I love your name."

"Oh, thank you..."

He paused so that she could offer her own.

"How do you know Alberto, Jack?"

"You mean Alberto our host? Actually, it's my cousin who knows him; she brought me here."

"You've never met him?"

"Nope, I only just met him tonight. And now you too..."

He waited again for her name. She held a sip on her tongue for an extra moment, still staring into his eyes. As if it was him she tasted.

Why wouldn't she give him her name? She must have told someone already; he'd seen other guests introduce themselves to her. But even Freddie might not know it. She would've rattled off the woman's biography to him if she did.

The woman moved close to him, laying her hand on his sleeve until he could feel the warmth from her fingertips against his own skin.

"Let's take one of these bottles out to the patio."

She stepped away and crossed the room, legs swinging like long swords. Jack grabbed a full bottle and followed through the tall glass doors, out of the air conditioning and into the thick, open night. She kept her head up and steady, like she was used to being stared at, as she led him to the back of the patio and waited at a round stone table. But Jack drew next to her and noticed she'd brought them out of sight of anyone else on the patio, in the shadows of the strings of garden lights and behind a flowering tree.

"So, Jack Steiner-Casillas, you said you came with your cousin. Do you know anyone else here tonight?"

"Not really, no…"

Jack couldn't guess why she kept asking who he'd met. Did she wonder why he'd been standing alone?

"And you don't know my cousin, do you?"

She shook her head. Jack wrestled down frustration; he had to do better than tepid small talk. He spoke quickly.

"I want to say I've met you, too, but you haven't told me *your* name yet."

In the soft light, he saw a coolness settle across her face. Her eyes flickered away from him and swept over the patio. Jack had noticed it once already, like her brain ran scheduled scans of the area. The woman hesitated for another moment before she answered.

"Marilen."

Her body had turned tense; she watched Jack's eyes as she waited.

"Marilen…mucho gusto."

Jack wouldn't have blamed her if she'd crashed this party. Stout, middle-aged Alberto had a tropical palace of a house, he offered up booze like it would never run out, and one of the guests had pulled into the driveway in a Maserati. But she wasn't just a rando sneaking in; too many people kept walking right up to her. And most of the time, within minutes she'd walk right off in another direction.

No, she had to want to avoid somebody.

Marilen picked up the bottle and refilled his glass.

"Is this your first time in Panamá?"

"Oh no, I've been coming here every year. Since I was a baby. I guess my accent gives it away that I'm American, huh?"

Her mouth stiffened. She was trying not to laugh.

"That was part of it, yes...do you have family here, then?"

"Y-yeah, some relatives. My grandparents are from here, but my mom was born in Minneapolis...I love it here, though."

Jack swallowed more of his drink. Marilen couldn't have any real interest in him, a glaring rube and a poser. Talking to him helped her stay out of someone's sight. Her eyes flickered over the patio before settling back on him.

His shoulders and back tightened; he ran through guesses on why she needed to hide. Spreading rumors? Human trafficking? Tumblr fight?

"You must, if you come here every year."

"Oh god, yeah. Everything's so beautiful here, everywhere I look I see these like, these bursts of color from all the flowers. And the ocean, I love how it shimmers in the sunlight. I can just sit and watch the waves roll in for hours."

"And the people?"

"Yeah, for sure. People are great here, absolutely."

She stepped a little closer, running her fingers over a fold on his sleeve.

"You certainly dress like a Panamanian."

He blinked as if he'd been jerked awake. Marilen laid her whole hand on his arm.

"I know I told you already, but I love the sound of your name. Steiner-Casillas. It makes me think of music...those grand pianos."

Heat flowed up from her hand and rushed through Jack's blood.

"Really? You think I actually look I'm from Panamá?"

"I didn't realize you were American when I first saw you."

A smile broke across his face.

"Tell me, Jack...are you good at keeping secrets?"

He inhaled the smell of the tree's flowers drifting on a thick breeze. He rested his elbows on the table and leaned in until his head was inches from hers.

"Yes, I am."

"I've had a very hard week, I've had a lot of stress. I need to relax. Not for very long, just a quick moment to relax."

She nodded across the patio. On the other side of the swimming pool, he saw a detached cottage, the door lit by the pool's changing blue and purple lights.

"That's Alberto's guest house. There is no one there right now. Grab another bottle and meet me inside."

She drew her hand away, and something glinted. He tilted his eyes and fixed on the gold band on her finger.

Somehow, he'd never thought she might be married. All his nerves disappeared, and Jack exhaled.

"Are you really sure? Even though…"

He nodded toward her hand. Marilen let it stay on the table and gave him a girlish, almost embarrassed smile.

"I'm only human."

She turned and moved across the dark path to the pool before Jack could ask anything more.

He waited for a moment by himself in the dark, rubbing his forehead, almost dazed. He'd let his cousin and sister tease him until he was so worked up he couldn't think. Until the idea that a woman would speak discreetly because she sold humans into slavery would hit him before the idea that she just had a husband. He'd acted clueless and deserved to get laughed at.

No, not clueless. Obviously not; a gorgeous, poised woman wanted to spend the party with him. He took long strides back to the house for another bottle.

Midnight fireworks cracked over the neighborhood as Jack ambled out of the guest house's glass doors and onto the grass. Marilen had slipped out first, almost ten minutes before, sliding back into her violet dress and composed posture, and giving him a goodbye kiss on the cheek. He walked with his head in a glowing fog that smelled of sweet wine and her perfume.

He stepped back into the main house; the guests had thinned. He couldn't see Marilen anywhere. Her voice passed through his mind, her last request when her lips touched his skin.

Tonight will be our special secret, Jack Steiner-Casillas.

He sat back on a couch and rested his head. Across the living room, Alberto laughed with another guest, his grin broad and his face flushed. Jack straightened, fixing his gaze on objects and blinking, trying to settle his double vision. Why had Marilen asked him if he knew Alberto so quickly?

He took a quick breath; she'd appeared again, moving to Alberto's side. He laid a hand on her back and brought her forward. With her shoulders and chest held up, like a queen, she gave the other guest a greeting kiss on the cheek and a gracious smile.

Marilen had pulled away from every person at the party. She'd spoken with Jack out of sight because he was the only one who didn't know Alberto.

He was the only one who didn't know Marilen was Alberto's wife.

A heaviness hit him, and his heartbeat flowed in his ears. This was how it felt to waltz into a man's house, pour down his booze, and make his wife moan your name.

"Jacky. Hey, Jacky!"

Someone tapped his cheek; Freddie, snapping her fingers in his face and giggling.

"Wake up, we're heading out."

Jack's heart rate slowed. All the guests were as festive as before, and Marilen didn't look at him. No one knew. For all he could guess, Alberto didn't even care how his wife had fun.

The warm fog gathered again around his head. His Spanish was sloppy, and he didn't really understand water conservation laws. But another man's elegant Panamanian wife did still want to stroke his hips and legs with firm fingers.

"Arright, if you say so…"

He pushed himself up and followed his cousin to the

door, where Lola waited. Freddie turned back and giggled again.

"Well, *you* sure look like you enjoyed yourself. What are you grinning about?"

"Nothing, no reason."

Jack woke up when he felt strong sunlight on his forehead. He turned his heavy, tight head away and kept his eyes shut, reminding himself of the cab ride that brought them back to Freddie's apartment. Marilen's deep, sultry smile passed through his mind.

His cousin and sister were already up. For a while, maybe, considering how loud and fast their voices sounded. He dragged himself off the bed and stepped out of the guest room he slept in, guzzling water from the hall bathroom sink.

"You okay?"

He'd forgotten to close the door; Lola watched him from the hall in a T-shirt and pajama shorts, a strange, alert look on her face. He nodded.

"Yeah, I'm good. I just got up. Here, I'll get outta your way."

He wiped his mouth with a towel and stepped out of the bathroom, moving down the hall. Lola followed him instead of entering the bathroom.

"Did you hear us in there?"

"Yeah, but it's no big deal, I needed to get up any-ways."

"No, I meant about last night."

"Last night? Huh, I don't know...all I know is I'm not so clueless that I don't know how to eat a woman out."

Apparently, Lola was too surprised to respond. Jack didn't hide his grin, but he tried to come up with a snappier line for Freddie. He reached the kitchen and saw her pacing in front of the TV, talking fast on the phone.

While a news reporter talked in Spanish in the background, a photograph of Marilen's smiling face hovered on the screen.

"Wait...what's going on?"

He turned back to his sister; now she stared at him, shocked and baffled.

"Lola, why is Marilen on TV?"

He heard an edge in his own voice. Freddie ended her call and came closer to him, the same nervous energy as Lola in her eyes.

"Seems like no one knows yet what actually happened, but last night, after the party...Alberto threw her out a window."

Something smashed his chest.

"W-what?"

"I'm still trying to figure it out, but it sounds like there was a fight..."

Jack grabbed the sides of his head as the blood drained from his brain, filling up his ears. The photo of Marilen— that very posed photo, of Marilen in a suit from the shoulders up—switched to video. She passed along a gathered crowd, shaking hands.

"Why is she...why she doing that?"

Freddie looked at the TV, then turned back to him, concern in her eyes.

"What? Being at a rally last month? Why wouldn't she?"

He swallowed, working harder to keep speaking.

"What did she do?"

"What d'you mean, what did—wait, Jacky, do you not know who she *was?*"

Jack had watched her turn away from every guest who knew her. She had chosen him, but not because he didn't know her husband.

"She said her name was Marilen…"

Lola stepped closer.

"Yeah, we talked about her yesterday. Maria Elena Navarro. The representative with the water conservation laws."

Because he was the only one clueless enough not to recognize her.

"I mean, for Christ's sake, her campaign billboard on the Amador Causeway has her *face* on it—Jacky!"

He pitched forward. Freddie and Lola caught him somewhere before the floor and held him up under his arms, moving him while his legs just shuffled. He was let down on a couch cushion; they both begged him to say he was alright.

He heard them yelling at each other. He tried to croak at them.

"What's, uh, what's going to happen to the water law?"

TURISTAS
HECTOR ACOSTA

By Olivia's count, there were twenty of them tonight.

They sat and waited; their backs draped with the glow of the headlights from rusted trucks. Last minute stragglers broke through the white tint, directed to join the group by a bored-looking Mexican who stood on the sidelines, the handle of a silver gun peeking from his waistband. People grumbled and made room for the newcomers, trying to be mindful of the toritos scattered on the ground. The nasty little burrs were a staple of the Southwest desert, hitching rides via the clothes and skin of anyone who didn't watch where they walked. Olivia was almost done plucking away at the few clinging to the cuff of her jeans when the flaquita squeezed next to her. Smoothing the long, white floral dress she wore, the pretty girl turned to the boy to her right and said, "Es mi primera vez cruzando la frontera."

It was her first time crossing the border.

"Está bien fácil," the boy said, looking the girl up and down as if attempting to divine what lied underneath the fabric of her dress.

"Really?" Black bands formed around the girl's finger

as she played with her hair.

"Sí," the boy nodded. "Just make sure to watch your stuff. I wouldn't trust anyone here." Leaning forward, he added, "But if anyone starts giving you trouble, just tell me, nothing here I can't handle."

Olivia rolled her eyes. This vato here, with his collared shirt, clean white sneakers, and gold-rimmed sunglasses atop slick-back hair was a fresa through and through. Just some upper-class brat from the other side of the border who decided to spend a Saturday night slumming it with the common folk.

La flaca bought it, though. Scooching her ass closer to the boy, she said, "I'm Veronica."

"Pedro."

The orange flame of a lighter sparked in the night, stretching the shadows like masa being pulled and rolled into new shapes. Before long, the smell of weed hung in the air, adding an undesired weight to Olivia's thoughts. When the joint reached her, she considered the rolled paper for a second before passing it to the bearded gringo behind her.

Around her, people fiddled with their phones, their fingers sliding across devices as messages were sent back and forth, slowed down only by the spotty cell phone reception. Strands of English and Spanish weaved together, people discussing weekend plans, dates they'd been on, and the latest chismos.

"Enough with the talking."

El Coyote stepped forward, the black ski mask blending his features into the night and muffling his Norteño accent. An AK-47 was slung on his shoulder in a manner so casual, Olivia imagined him in front of a mirror, practicing poses until he found the perfect one. Two things kept him from coming off like the mero chingon he so clearly wanted to be. First, the camo shirt he wore didn't cover his panza, giving everyone a glimpse of a belly button mired in coarse black hair. More importantly, Olivia knew the gun to be nothing but a cheap plastic toy, bought at the mercado and painted black.

Pacing back and forth, El Coyote started his speech, describing the dangerous journey they were about to embark on. He warned everyone of la migra, reminding them to keep their eyes and ears open. He spoke of the narcos in a hushed tone, telling them of the drug gangs that had taken over entire swaths of Mexico and who, according to El Coyote, could be lying in wait for them even now. He ended his speech with talk of Los Estados Unidos, the promised land. Of the families waiting to be reunited, of the jobs and the riches they would all know, long as they were willing to work hard to get there.

It was a good speech, Olivia thought, delivered with a conviction that pulled the crowd away from their phones and conversations. The mood tilted, a vibration jumping from person to person as the anticipation built. Looking at the eager faces around her, brown and white, Olivia regretted having passed on the joint. She watched the crowd nod along to El Coyote's words and marveled at how all these people came out and willingly paid one thousand pesos for a true-to-life border experience.

Five hundred if, like Olivia, you remembered to use the Groupon.

Las Caminatas had been around for a couple of years now, the first tours set up by townsfolks in pueblitos far away from any actual borders, where turistas dripping in suntan lotion and carrying around fanny packs were charged a couple of dollars to walk around the desert until they tired themselves out. It was something to do by those who wanted to go back home and brag about how they didn't just eat tacos and visit the zocalo on their trip here.

With interest in the border at an all-time high, it wasn't long before enterprising folks started expanding on the original idea. They added extras routes, props, and most important of all, actors playing key roles. There was The Coyote, tasked with navigating everyone across the border, the narcotraficantes waiting to rob the group with toy guns and plastic knives, and the Border Patrol agents driving beat-up camionetas jury-rigged with flashing lights.

The tours drew in all types of people, Olivia had learned. There were those who came with a need to understand what family and friends went through as they made their journeys Norte. Others arrived saddled with the guilt of being born on the right side of the border, convinced two hours of walking in the desert would be penance enough. And some simply came out of curiosity.

"We didn't feel comfortable with Tommy going over there, you see," the mother had told Olivia. The woman's hair was piled high in a concha-like bun, and Olivia feared it would topple over as she spoke. Her makeup was carefully applied, giving the woman a plastic, Barbie-doll sheen. Her husband sat stiffly next to her, dressed in a business suit and looking like he'd rather be anywhere other than the small taqueria Olivia had told them to meet her in. Both looked like they came out straight out of a telenovela. "You just hear all sorts of horrible stories of what's going on in Mexico," the woman continued, not bothering to touch el caldo de pollo she ordered. "No offense," she'd quickly added.

Olivia had waved the offense away with one hand and picked up a taco al pastor off her plate with the other. She'd never looked for a missing kid before, but La Dueña Reyna had been bugging her about the rent for a few days now and besides, how hard could it be? El gringito probably pissed off the wrong cop and was now sitting in some Mexican jail cell waiting to be bailed out.

Except he wasn't. Nor was he one of the seven cadavers she'd seen at the morgue throughout the weeks. And if he'd visited La Mariscal, none of the girls walking the streets and flashing tits at the slowed-down traffic remembered him. After a couple of days of fruitless searching, she was steered toward the tours by one of Tommy's friends. Tommy, she was told, had been trying to convince the friend to take the tour with him, to no avail. "Why would I pay to walk in the desert for a couple of hours?" Tommy's friend had asked her. This question led her to La Caminata's constantly updated social media page, full of pictures and tweets of people's experiences with the tour. It took some time and scrolling, but eventually she found Tommy's tweet. It was a picture he'd posted of himself staring straight ahead at the camera, the desert behind him. Tommy had thick eyebrows and small green eyes. Fat clung to his cheeks and dropped the look of his age, while pale whispers of hair were scattered across his chin in a style so random Olivia didn't know whether the kid had missed them while shaving or just didn't care. But it was the hat sitting atop Tommy's shaggy hair that Olivia focused on.

Tommy, it turned out, was a red hat.

A click through his social media account verified it. It

was a churn of ignorance and the type of spiel usually found plastered on a truck's bumper sticker. His posts were written in all capital letters and were full of praise toward a president obsessed with building a wall. The kid's own tweets decried everything from immigrants to the girls at school who ignored him. Olivia wished she could have dropped the job right then and there, but the money had already been paid to Dueña Reyna, and there was still the matter of next month's rent.

"Solo un poquito mas, and we'll be at the border," El Coyote said, dropping Spanish and English words in his sentence, like an indecisive eater at a buffet line.

She'd been trying to get to El Coyote all evening, but the man refused to slow down. When he wasn't at the head of the group, promising they were this close to reaching the border, he mingled among the tourists, flirting with the girls and allowing them to hold his gun, or telling the Americans, which there were plenty, about the close calls he'd had at the border—back when "he did this for the real."

"You think he knows he's pointing in the wrong direction?" muttered a woman trudging up the same hill as Olivia. She was short, wearing a pair of dusty blue jeans and a black windbreaker to shield her from the cold temperatures that had taken by surprise many of the people around them.

"Is he?" Olivia asked, even though she knew that already.

The woman turned her flashlight westward. "El Paso is that way, vez?"

Olivia did see, the woman's flashlight pointing directly at the Franklin Mountains, and below them, the winking lights of the border city that lay on the U.S. side of the border.

"Almost as if this whole thing is fake," Olivia said.

Leaning forward, the woman whispered, "That gun of his isn't even real."

Olivia gasped. "No! Next, you're going to tell me las luchas aren't real either."

The woman laughed, a deep, throaty sound that caused her cheeks to ripple. Tommy started to become a distant second thought. "I'm Olivia."

"Teresa." The woman switched her flashlight to her left hand and extended her right one to Olivia.

"Are you enjoying La Caminata?" Olivia asked.

"¡Claro! Nothing I love more than walking aimlessly around the desert while a guy with a power complex screams at me."

"Kind of amazing, isn't it?" Olivia asked.

"What is?"

"The way we've turned what our people go through into a Disney ride, like something out of Los Mojados de los Caribbean. All for the entertainment of people like those over there," Olivia said, pointing to Pedro. The boy and girl who sat next to her at the start of the tour walked a couple of feet ahead of them now, focused on each other rather than anything El Coyote was saying. Pedro's arms were wrapped around the girl's waist and often trended downwards, much to the giggles, squeals, but very little fight from the girl—Veronica, Olivia remembered her name was. Others around the couple either talked amongst themselves or stopped and grouped together to take selfies. Olivia figured the photos would end up in social media as soon as they had decent cell phone reception. Hashtag LA FRONTERA, hashtag CROSSING THE BORDER.

"There's worse things than folks making money off the interest in our border," Teresa said. "When you think about it, es puro Mexicano what's happening here. It's what we've always done—make the best of a shitty situation."

"We should be trying to change the shitty situation."

"Del dicho al hecho, gran trecho," Teresa said, her flashlight flickering. She hit it on the side with the palm of her hand until the beam held shape. "So, why are you here, Olivia?"

"Curiosidad," Olivia answered. Somewhere ahead, she could hear the murmur of the rest of their group, El Coyote's words of encouragement rolling through the darkness. She tried to keep her focus on the man, but Teresa's presence kept pulling at her attention like a child pulling the tail of a cat.

"¿Y? Has your curiosity been satisfied?" Teresa asked.

Before Olivia could answer, she spotted El Coyote breaking away from the group of tourists and heading out by himself. Olivia turned to Teresa and said, "I have to go." She tried to keep the disappointment out of her voice.

Blinking, Teresa tilted her head at Olivia, hair cascading down one side of her face and pooling around her shoulder. "Fue un placer," she said, her eyes tugging at Olivia and making her want to stay.

Glancing behind her, she saw the disappearing shape of El Coyote heading into the desert. "Maybe I'll run into you again before La Caminata ends."

"That'd be nice," Teresa said, still looking at her.

Olivia broke her gaze, afraid that if she didn't, she would remain at the woman's side. She turned and hurried in the same direction as El Coyote, Teresa's face fluttering on the edges of her mind.

* * *

El Coyote was humming the opening bars of a popular corrido, his back turned to Olivia.

His legs were spread wide, the gun laying on the ground beside him. As Olivia neared, she heard piss hitting the ground. She waited until his stream turned into a trickle and placed her hand on the man's shoulder. El Coyote gave a startled shout and turned around, moving so fast he almost tripped on his own feet. Olivia grabbed him by the arm and kept him balanced.

He'd taken off the ski mask, revealing gaunt cheeks and a pushed-in nose, the tip of it sprouting a field of blackheads. His skin had gone too many rounds with the sun and now looked as if it would crinkle and fold upon itself if the man smiled. "Chingado, casi me das un attaque," he said.

"¿Como van las cosas, Alejandro?"

At the sound of his name, Alejandro stopped checking his pants for wet spots and looked up. "¿Te conosco?"

"No, but you know Paco."

Paco was an old friend of hers, un borracho from the neighborhood who knew everyone and their business. Olivia had gone to him for info on the tours, and it had only taken three cups of café negro for him to dribble out Alejandro's name as someone she should talk to.

"Which Paco?" Alejandro asked, zipping up his fly.

"El de la colonia," Olivia said. "He said you two used to go out drinking at La Paloma."

"That Paco? I haven't seen that guy in years. How's he doing?"

"Igual que siempre."

"So, drunk then," Alejandro said, reaching down to pick his gun off the ground. "And why was Paco telling you about me, muñeca?"

"I'm looking for someone, and he thought you might be able to help."

"Yeah?" Alejandro threw her a grin, and Olivia suddenly understood why he wore the mask.

"Sorry," Olivia said, "but that's not what I'm looking for. Besides, looked to me like you had enough attention back there, way those girls flocked to you for pictures."

"One of the perks of the job," Alejandro said and looked at her. "You look familiar. Have I seen you before?"

He might have. This was Olivia's third Caminata, all of them with Alejandro as The Coyote. She chose to keep that to herself. "I don't think so."

"¿Como te llamas?"

"Olivia."

"And you sure we haven't met?"

"Maybe I just have that type of face." Taking her phone out, Olivia flipped through her pictures until she found Tommy's. "You recognize him?" she asked.

Alejandro didn't even shift his eyes to the photo. "Nope."

Rolling her eyes, Olivia pushed the phone toward the man. "Come on, look again."

Alejandro pushed the phone away. "I see tons of kids each night. After a while, they all start to look the same. White or brown, that's the only difference."

Undeterred, Olivia followed him. "This one made the news, though. He's been missing for a couple of weeks now."

"Que sorpresa," Alejandro said. "One of theirs get lost, and everyone is out buscándolo." He glanced to Olivia and added, "Even have one of us looking for him."

Ignoring the barb, Olivia pressed on. "What's the hurry, Alejandro? I'm pretty sure the kids waiting to buy your stuff will still be there when you get back."

"No sé de que hablas," Alejandro said, staring straight ahead.

But Olivia caught the quick flash in her direction when she uttered the accusation. He knew exactly what she was talking about. Pressing on, she continued, "I couldn't figure out at first," Olivia said, matching his walk. "Why there's so many chiquillos taking the tour. Or why they treat you like a celebrity, all of them asking for selfies and group photos. I find it hard to believe they've all taken a deep interest in border crossings."

Alejandro continued to avoid looking at Olivia and started to walk faster.

"You want to tell me what you got in those plastic baggies you keep passing to them?"

"No te metas en mis asuntos." Mind your business, he was telling her.

"Here's the thing," Olivia said, stepping in front of him. "It is my business. 'Cause right now, you're about the only person who I think can point me in the right direction. And if you don't, I guess I'll go to *El Diario* and tell them about your side job. Don't imagine your bosses would be too happy to find out you've been selling drugs to all the young American tourists back there."

The truth was, the only person she knew at *El Diario* was the guy who called her up and told her they were cancelling her newspaper delivery for lack of payment, but she figured Alejandro didn't need to know that.

"It's only a little weed and pills," Alejandro muttered, dropping the macho act just as quickly as he dropped his shoulders. "Most of them are already getting harder stuff on their own."

"You think your bosses would buy that?"

"¿Que quieres?" he asked, now looking like an unmolded piece of clay.

Olivia handed him her phone. "Tell me if you remember the kid."

Alejandro looked down at the photo on the phone and made a face. "Yeah, I remember this pendejo." He tapped on the screen. "He was wearing this gorra too. You say he's gone missing? Good."

"Must have been a surprise to see a guy like that here."

"We get them every so often, cabrones wanting to prove how easy the walk is, or who think the whole thing is real and that we're using this as another way to sneak in a bunch of Mexicans across the border."

"What you do with them?"

"What do you think? We take their money," Alejandro said. He must have seen the surprised look on Olivia's face, because he added, "Most of them are harmless. Bien chiflados, but harmless."

"¿No te enojas?" Olivia wanted to know. "Doesn't it make you angry to be around them? To know what they think of us?"

Shrugging, Alejandro said, "They're going to think it either way, right? So why not at least take their money? Y no somos estupidos. Any of them who even look like they're going to start trouble, we kick them right out."

"Did Tommy get out of line?"

"Not with me he didn't. El niño just hung back most of the time. I think he was waiting for one of us to start shit with him or something. He had his phone out the whole damn time, filming and taking pictures."

"Any idea why he was here?"

"Like I said, he kept mostly to himself." Glancing to the direction they both came from, Alejandro checked his watch and said, "He probably wanted to brag to all his racist friends that he did it."

Olivia remembered what she'd heard about Tommy pressing his friend to join him for the tour. "When's the last time you saw him?"

"I don't know! If it wasn't for that stupid red hat, I probably wouldn't even remember him at all." Alejandro looked like he was going to walk off before getting a strange look on his face. "Ya me acorde. I saw him around the halfway point."

Olivia knew the tour lasted about three hours, so that would have been around the hour and a half mark. "What was he doing?"

"Talking to one of our girls. I don't think it was for more than a few minutes, but it stuck with me."

"Why?"

"Because of how he was acting around her. I remember thinking that if all the red gorras got laid by a brown girl, there wouldn't be any talk about the wall anymore."

Olivia tried not to gag, or punch Alejandro. "You know the girl?"

"I already told you, one of ours, and I only saw them talking for a few minutes."

"Either of them finished the tour?"

"No te puedo decir. By the end of the tour, I'm more interest in going home than making sure everyone cross."

"You guys don't do a head count? Keep records to make sure no one gets lost?"

Alejandro laughed. "Yeah, sure, and we also make you to give everyone bottled water and fancy sandwiches. Listen, as long as no one is crying too much by the end, we call it a successful night and go home." He started to put his mask back on. "And I have to go now. We done here?"

Olivia studied him, looking for those small signs she came across daily, the twitches and fidgeting that told her someone was lying. But El Coyote did none of those. Olivia believed him. "Yeah, go," she said, wondering what she would do now.

"You ever heard of La Llorona?" Teresa asked.

Olivia nodded. Every Mexican knew the story of the woman who'd lost her children and now walked all of Mexico, wailing, "¡Ay, mis hijos!" eternally cursed to search for those who would never be found.

"My mom told me that story whenever we went out in public," Teresa said. "She used to say, "Mija, La Llorona isn't picky; she'll take you if she sees you.""

She'd come across Teresa not long after returning to the group, and now both sat together on an uncluttered piece of desert, Olivia stretching her legs while Teresa sat cross-legged next to her. Teresa's knee would occasionally graze against Olivia's thigh as she talked, sending small shivers through Olivia whenever it happened.

"It was El Cucuy for me. Every night my dad would tuck me in and tell me if I misbehaved, I'd be dragged out of bed by my feet and become un antojito for it."

The rest of the group stood a few feet away, listening to Alejandro as he pointed to a nearby tree. The only vegetation in miles, the tree broke through the desert soil, its gnarled, skinny branches stretching outwards rather than upward as if resigned with the knowledge it could never touch the sky. Hanging from the branches were a wide variety of women's underwear, in all sizes and colors. Some of them were draped across the branches like wet clothes on a laundry line, their fabric stretched and frayed, while others hung listlessly from their elastic bands like the strangest of Christmas garland.

"Pongan atención," El Coyote started off, his voice carrying all the way to where Olivia and Teresa sat. "Not every Coyote can be trusted. There are men who will lead the women out to spots like this with lies or by gunpoint so that they can claim them as their own. Afterward, they hang their underwear off trees exactly like this one, as a reminder that el desierto toma lo que desea."

"Un montón de mentiras," Teresa said, flicking some of the toritos that had accumulated around the tops of Olivia's sock at the crowd's direction. "Those trees are as real as La Llorona and El Cucuy and at least those two are our own creations." Anger lined her words, sharp and clear in the night.

Olivia listened to Teresa and watched the crowd snap pictures of the tree, wondering if it or El Coyote's words would be remembered by any of them as they crossed the bridge back home after the tour.

"Are you still going to look for the gringo?" Teresa asked, looking down at Tommy's picture on Olivia's phone.

"I don't know. A lo mejor." Olivia rubbed one of the picked-off burrs between her fingers, its sharp hooks pressing against her skin until it broke through and drew blood. She'd told Teresa of her search for Tommy as they'd walked to the tree, describing her time in Juarez hunting down leads and following trails. Showed her the countless text messages she had with his friends, most of whom hadn't talked to Tommy in the days prior to his disappearance. Olivia hadn't meant to tell her as much as she did, but halfway through the story she realized how nice it was to let out a whole week's worth of frustrations.

Plus, Teresa loved it. She was enamored with the idea of Olivia as a detective and even told her she would look good in a trench coat and hat. The only thing Teresa didn't care for was Tommy himself. Soon as Olivia told her about him being a red hat, she, like Alejandro, thought it was a good thing he went missing.

"Maybe La Llorona took him," Teresa said.

"Maybe," Olivia said, thinking at this point that was as good of a theory as any. Silence stretched between them like a cat basking in warm sunlight.

"Okay," Teresa said suddenly, "we know our Tomás went missing somewhere in this tour, right?"

"That's what I'd been thinking all along. But now I'm wondering if I was wrong. Who's to say he didn't complete the tour and go somewhere else?"

"We should try to see if we can figure out who that girl El Coyote mentioned was. See if she remembers something that Alejandro doesn't."

Tilting her head, Olivia asked, "We? I thought you said maybe it was a good thing he went missing."

"Oh, come on!" Teresa moved closer to Olivia; her lips drawn upwards in a smile. "Solving a mystery is a lot more interesting than this." She waved her arm around them.

Having finished his lecture, El Coyote clapped his hands together and announced, "You all got five more minutes before we start walking again. Con ganas."

Staring at El Coyote, Olivia replayed their conversation for what felt like the millionth time, turning and twisting everything he said as she attempted to find a different angle, something she'd missed the first time around. She was so focused on the task that it wasn't until Teresa shook her shoulder that she snapped and turned to look at her.

"I've been calling your name for the last few minutes," Teresa said.

"Sorry."

"Did you ever go through all of La Caminata's pictures on their social media account?" Teresa asked.

"Yeah, I think so. That's the only one I found of Tommy, though."

"I went through them right now—the reception here is probably the best it's been all night—and I think I found something."

"Another picture of Tommy?"

Teresa shook her head and passed the phone back to Olivia, "No, something else. See." She pointed to the picture she had up on the screen. It showed a group of tourists sitting cross-legged on the desert ground, while above them, three Mexicans pointed fake guns at them.

"What am I looking for?" Olivia asked.

"Just wait," Teresa said and slid her finger across the phone, replacing the current photo with a new one. It was a shot of five tourists after having crossed the border. She knew this because in the background there was a large banner that read "UNITED STATES."

"I still don't..."

Teresa replaced the photo one more time. This one featured La Caminata's version of the migra—two men and a woman in black uniforms standing next to a Jeep while a couple of tourists stood in a line, their hands pressed together with zip cuffs.

Olivia was about to say she still didn't know what Teresa wanted her to find when she saw it. Or thought she saw it. Standing up, she gripped the phone, focusing on the woman playing the role of the border patrol agent. She looked familiar. Heart racing, she went back to the second photo, scanning the group who crossed the border and stopping when she saw the same woman. Back to the first photo Teresa had shown her. Now knowing what to look for, she spotted the woman immediately, this time as one of the Mexicans holding the gun.

It was Veronica. The one who'd been quick to cling to the boy and said it was her first time doing the tours.

"I remember her from the start of the tour," Olivia explained to Teresa as they walked through the desert, moving away from the path the rest of the group was taking. "She was already working on a guy—Pedro, I think he said his name was."

She should have spotted Veronica in all those photos when she went through La Caminata's social media account. Now she couldn't help but wonder if Veronica had been part of any of the tours Olivia had previously been in. If the girl had gotten close to an American boy every time. Or if she waited until she found the right one. Like Tommy.

"Alejandro told me that Tommy had been speaking to a girl— 'one of ours,' he put it. At first, I thought he meant another Mexican. But he meant another employee of the tour, an actor."

Sure enough. Alejandro had confirmed as much to them. "She's pretty new," he'd told them in between trading money for baggies from the kids who came up to him. He'd also told them the last time he saw her; she and Pedro had been walking away from the group in the direction Teresa and Oliva were headed toward. "I figured she wanted to have some fun," Alejandro had said.

"I think I see someone," Teresa said and pointed straight ahead.

"Be careful," Olivia said.

"You don't think she's dangerous, do you?"

Olivia chewed on her inner cheek and didn't answer. As they got closer, a shape split from the black of the desert night and formed a slim figure.

"Hola!" Olivia shouted, raising her hand up toward the figures.

The figure turned, and Olivia recognized the dress and long hair as belonging to Veronica. She held a slim black flashlight on her left hand, her other hand holding on to a small and simple handbag. She stared at Olivia and Teresa as they approached her.

"Hola," Olivia tried again before adding, "Veronica?"

"¿Quién eres?" Veronica asked, aiming her flashlight up at them.

The light slammed into Olivia and almost made her stumble backward, right into Teresa. Shielding her eyes, she said, "Alejandro sent us to find you."

"Alejandro?"

"He said something about needing you back at the tour," Teresa said, using the lie they'd agreed on.

The flashlight turned off, enveloping them into the black of the desert again. After a couple of blinks, Olivia's vision returned, and she could now see Veronica standing stiffly before them, like a pole planted deep into the roots of the desert. Her dress hung slack off her shoulders and draped down all the way to the ground, the fabric unmoved by wind or motion.

"Who are you?" Veronica asked.

Olivia introduced herself and Teresa. "I'm a friend of Alejandro," she added.

"And he sent you." Veronica's tone of voice was as dry as the air, lacking any trace of the girl Olivia had witnessed sidle up to Pedro earlier that evening.

"Yeah, but he said there were two of you. A boy named Pedro, I think?" Olivia said, peering around and behind Veronica but seeing no one else.

"Ese se fue," Veronica said, pointing to the direction Olivia and Teresa had come from. "He left and went back to the tour."

"And left you here all alone? That seems kinda rude."

"Believe me, it was my choice to see him go. Se puso bien tocón," Veronica said.

Strange how she didn't seem to mind him getting all grabby on her earlier in the walk, Olivia thought, then instantly felt regret. Had she just slut-shamed this girl, all because she wanted to find a racist little kid?

"What does Alejandro want me for, anyways?"

"He didn't tell me," Olivia said.

"Funny, you think he would, right?" Veronica asked.

"I guess." Olivia watched Veronica carefully. Something about the way the girl was acting bothered her. She'd changed her act so quickly and seamlessly, like a change of clothes. Out of the corner of her eye, Olivia spotted Teresa bending down and picking something off the ground.

A pair of gold-rimmed sunglasses.

Veronica must have seen it too, because she whirled around and with an unexpected quickness, stepped toward

Teresa and grabbed her wrist. Already, Olivia was moving forward, her hand gripping the end of her flashlight and preparing to use it as a baton if she had to. "Let her go."

"Who are you both?" Veronica asked, still holding on to Teresa's wrist and twisting her arm as she put herself behind Teresa. "Y la verdad."

The grunt of pain that escaped from Teresa threatened to blanket Olivia's mind and bring a field of red with it. "¡Déjala ir!" Olivia shouted again. Her hand trembled, slightly afraid of what she would do if Veronica didn't let Teresa go.

"Not until you tell me who you are and what you're doing here." Veronica's voice had lost the tilt once more, returning to the more monotone voice she'd been using earlier.

"We told you, Alejandro sent us to get you." This came from Teresa, who continued to struggle. Veronica had to drop her purse and use her hand to grab Teresa's other wrist.

"Liar," Veronica said, twisting Teresa's arm behind her arm.

"I'm looking for someone!" Olivia shouted. "A guy in a red hat who took this tour a couple of weeks ago. I think you talked to him."

Veronica eyed Olivia. "Why?" she asked. "Why are you looking for him?"

"Because his family is paying me to."

"You don't look like a cop."

"I'm not," Olivia said and inched forward, "I'm—" she almost said detective before finishing with, "someone who finds things."

"Even assholes?"

"Especially assholes. They're the ones who go missing the most."

And maybe Veronica agreed, because she laughed. But still held on to Teresa. "He honestly believed everything that came out of his mouth, you know. Told me straight to my face how Mexico was so broken that he didn't really blame us for wanting to leave it, but it didn't mean he would allow it."

"Yeah, that sounds like the guy I'm looking for," Olivia said.

"That guy from tonight, Pedro, he wasn't much better. Told me he came here from El Paso because he heard we Mexican girls would give it up for a couple of dollar bills. And he's not the first. To most of the men, we're either their sirvientas or whores."

"What did you do with Tommy?"

"I finally couldn't take it anymore and told him that if he really felt it was as easy as he was making it out to be, then he should prove it."

"Please let Teresa go," Olivia said.

To her surprise, Veronica did just that, taking a step back and shoving Teresa toward Olivia. Teresa stumbled, but Olivia was there to catch her before she could fall to the ground, wrapping arms around the woman and pulling her away from Veronica.

"Are you okay?" she asked her.

Teresa took a deep breath and slowly nodded. Then she glanced back to Veronica. "You sent him out to the desert."

Veronica smiled at the two of them. "I didn't send him anywhere. He wanted to go."

"And him?" Olivia asked, pointing to the sunglasses that somehow Teresa had managed to hold on to the entire time. "Is he out there somewhere too?"

"I already told you, he went back to the tour." Another smile.

She was lying and wasn't even bothering to hide it, Olivia realized. Veronica knew they didn't have anything on her. She wondered how many times she'd done something like this, how many times she found a guy doing the tours who would do anything she said all because of a flutter of her eyelashes and a "por favor."

"I guess I should be heading back to the tour," Veronica said. "What with Alejandro needing me and all."

Olivia couldn't let it end like this. She gripped the flashlight tighter, her mind racing to figure out what she could do to stop Veronica from leaving.

"Olivia, look," Teresa said, pointing to Veronica's purse.

The purse was laying on the ground between the three of them. Open and on its side, it looked like roadkill taking its last breath. It had spilled its contents around the ground: a lip gloss, a single earring, loose change, and a bunch of small baggies, all full of multicolored pills—a rainbow of quick highs.

Like the ones Olivia had seen El Coyote sell all night long.

"You didn't just dare Tommy to walk to El Paso. You gave him something first. Probably whatever you could buy from Alejandro. This place is difficult enough with all your senses intact. If you were high and walking at night—"

"He would have never made it, "Teresa finished for her.

"I'm thinking that's what you did with Pedro tonight too. You gave him some of the drugs and pushed him into the night. Maybe told him that if he made it all the way across the border, you would find him and reward him.

All while knowing the drugs would make sure he never got there."

Veronica shifted from foot to foot, ignoring the baggies. Instead, she glanced toward the direction of El Paso and folded her arms. "I don't know what you're talking about."

"Bullshit," Olivia said. "You sentenced them both to their deaths doing that. I want to know why."

"Let's say I did. Between us girls and the desert, would two missing Americanos really be the worst thing in the world? Especially boys like Tommy and Pedro? Both looking down at us unless they can use us or fuck us. Who cares if they go missing? Maybe more of them should."

"It's not up to you to decide that though," Olivia said.

"Why not? Over on their side, you have a bunch of men who think they can do whatever they want with us. Separating families and feeding children to a system that doesn't care for them."

"Is that why you did this?" Olivia asked. "For revenge?"

"She did it because of La Llorona," Teresa spoke up and took a step toward Veronica.

Olivia turned to look at her. "Teresa, what are you doing?"

Teresa ignored her and kept talking as she walked toward Veronica. "Lloronas. All of them walking through life, crying for their missing children. And no one seems to give one puta." Her voice cracked and was unsteady for a moment. "Why shouldn't they feel what countless of us feel?" Reaching Veronica, Teresa placed a hand on her shoulder and asked, "Isn't that right?"

Through Teresa's entire walk and speech, Veronica had watched her, enthralled. It was only when Teresa touched her that the girl seemed to snap out of the trance. She slowly nodded.

"Vete," Teresa said gently and pushed Veronica in the direction of the tour.

"She can't leave, Teresa," Olivia said.

"Go," Teresa told Veronica, this time with more force. "Get back to the tour. Alejandro probably is actually looking for you by now."

Veronica started walking. She walked right past Olivia, close enough that Olivia could have grabbed the girl and stopped her if she wanted to, but she didn't, instead just looking at Teresa.

"We can't let her get away with this," Olivia said, even as she knew that's exactly what they were doing.

"¿Por qué no?" Teresa asked, not moving from her spot. "How many of them get away with something like this, and worse, every day? Damn it, Olivia, every hour."

"They were still someone's children. We could still find Pedro tonight and bring him back."

"Our flashlight isn't going to last much longer. If we start looking for him, we might be the ones who end up getting lost. Let's go back and end the tour, Olivia. Please."

Olivia's breaths came fast and shallow, her chest tightening as she processed Teresa's words. She thought of the people she'd seen taking the tour today, snapping pictures at the rape tree, giggling through El Coyote's stories of plight and hardship that people, real people, had gone through. And she thought of Veronica, having to do this every day, having to stare at a new batch of people making their way through a fake crossing for a couple of pesos a day, all while dealing with people like Tommy and Pedro.

She looked at Teresa, and then past her, toward the

lights of El Paso. The other side. Wondered how far Tommy had made it before the cold of the night or the heat of the day made him stumble and fall. Imagined Pedro doing the same right now, his mind clouded with the drugs.

Maybe Tommy had made it across the border. People did. And maybe Pedro was back at the tour, laughing and bragging at how he got with a real Mexican girl.

"Olivia? Can we go?"

Olivia closed her eyes and listened to the desert, hoping it would tell her what to do.

BOBO
RICHIE NARVAEZ

Hel-*lo-o! Dios te bendiga!* It's good to hear your voice.
Yeah, yeah, everybody's okay. When are you coming here?
We just got a new generator, and we got plenty of food
now. I don't know about cake. *Ja.* I know you like cake!
The bakery over here's still closed because *la tormenta de
la bruja Maria* put a car right through the kitchen, *tu
sabes.* But your Titi Blanca can fix you something, whatever you like. She is the chef of the house. Me, I just eat.
When's the last time you been here? Must be two, three
years. It's not as bad as it was right after *la tormenta de la
bruja Maria,* oh my god. *Pero, Dios aprieta pero no
ahoga.* You should have been here, *ja.*

But really, it's better, a lot better. The hospital over here
got a big donation. Everything is new there. There's still
lines for gas and for water, but it's not bad like it was. *No
te apures.* There's always a bed for you here. Hey, you
know your cousin Nick? He was just here. Hold on—

Blanca! BLANCA! When was Nicky here?—It's Raphael.
Mi sobrino!—*Tu sobrino, tambien.*—*Si,* the big one with the
glasses.—*Si, que le gusta bizcocho, ja ja.*—It was January,

right?—*Que?*—*QUE?!*—Nicky!—*Enero!*—*E-NE-RO!*—He was just here, right?—*Noviembre?* Right after the hurricane?—*Mujer, no me mientas*—*No me mientas, mujer*—wow—No!—Oh, yeah, that's right, that's right.—Before the police. That's right.—You're right.

She's right—the woman's always right. Don't forget that when you get married. When are you getting married? *Ja.* No, I'm just kidding! *Ja.*

Like I say, Nick, he was just here. My memory's not too good. I tell you: Don't get old. The last year has been terrible, *tu sabes*, terrible. I'm getting old. That's why you should come soon!

So, Nick, we hadn't seen him in ten, fifteen years. Hold on, let me ask—

Blanca!...BLANCA!—

Oh, she go to get the diesel. She be there all day. *'chacho.* So Nick, he just show up, he didn't tell us he was coming. *Pero,* the phones *no sirve pa' na'*, it works one day, then no, *tu sabes?* Anyway, we was surprise to see him.

What a funny guy. He had one big bag, and he knock on the door, and before he say "Hi" he say, "Who do I have to f to get a drink around here?"

I no recognize him almost. He's a big guy, *tu sabes*, all muscles, with tattoos here, tattoos there, even on the neck, *'chacho.* But he got green eyes just like his mother, God have her in heaven. I told him we got no ice today, did he still want a drink. He say, *"Muerto quiere misa, Tio Luis."* What a funny guy, that guy, oh boy.

He say he tried to rent a car but there had no cars. So he had to take a taxi from the airport and he pay two hundred dollars. *Two hundred!* What a big spender. But if you got it... *tu sabes?*

Nick say he needed to stay here. I say, "*Sí, claro que sí.*" Like I say, we got plenty of room. We had a few people here already right after the hurricane. We had your cousin Chuche and her husband, they lost their house, and then the neighbors Ana and Felix, and your Titi Inez, and Blanca's friend Adriana. They all lost their house. Adriana, she was sleeping in her car after her apartment got flooded, and Blanca saw her and tell her to come here. "You can't sleep in the car. That's not a way to live."

Oh, *y* Bobo was here, too. You remember Bobo! Blanca's baby brother. They call him that because when he was little, he put a dress on a pig, and the pig no like it. He's tall, big, with crazy hair and a big beard. You remember, you used to play with him when you were a kid. He would throw you like a football until you got too chubby.

Bobo, he live by himself up in the mountains. He's like a big kid, *tu sabes,* in his head. But he build a little house all by hisself for him and his goat, and he say the house stay up in the hurricane, but he came here, with his goat, Doña Olga Tañón, to see how we doing. Once he saw everyone staying here, he say he want to stay here to keep us safe. Imagine. Anyway, he didn't stay in the house, though, he sleep on the roof every night. With the dog and Olga Tañón.

So, Nick, when he came, we had a good time drinking and making jokes. We told him he can stay in the living room, and we put a pillow and blanket on the couch. But he laughed. I thought he told a joke, but I no understand. But he say, "No, no, no, I can't sleep on no couch. My back kill me." 'chacho, *pobrecito hombre.* He's a hard-working man.

Qué? Oh, no, no, I don't know his job.

BOBO

So, yeah, right away Ana and her husband Felix, they say, "Take our room, it's okay. We small people, we stay on the couch."

Nick, what a guy, right away he took twenty dollars and gave it to Felix, and Felix say, "No, no, 'sok."

And Nick say, "You say my money's no good? You don't want my f'ing money."

And Carlos say, "No, no, 'sok."

And Nick, he pushed the money into Carlos' pants. "Take the f'ing money."

Nick, what a guy, but his mouth, oh my god. Everything is f this and f that. Well, what can you do? He's from New York.

The next day Nick say he need a car. Blanca, right away, she say, "All the highways are close. You crazy, you can't go nowhere." That's how she is.

Nick say he wanted to take a tour. "To see what?" she say. "It all looks the same. Stay near the house. It's dangerous."

But he say he need a car, and no one can tell him no. I tell him we got the truck, but it's underneath the mango tree. It fell on top, smash everything, *lo rompio todito*. I told him the only car that work here belong to Adriana.

Adriana, she's young. Very pretty. Very smart. She went to *colegio, pero* she work at El Pollo Tropical because that's all they have. Ain't no work here.

So, Nick say, "How about it? I gotta rent your car. How much you want?" He say he give her twenty dollars a day.

She say, "You want it, you gotta pay." Because she saw how Nick was with money. She say, "Fifty dollars a day."

He say she was crazy, but he was smiling.

Then she say, but she got no gasoline.

So that day we all went to the lines. Blanca to get the water. Chuche and her husband went to get food. Nick say he go with Adriana, and Bobo want to go too because everywhere Adriana go, he want to go. I went with them to get the diesel for the generator.

The line was very long and went very slow.

So, Nick, "Hey, Bobo, you look the f'ing same forever. They tell me you live in the mountains. You got a goat for a wife? *Ja ja ja.*"

Nick, he always making jokes, always.

No, no, Bobo say, "I don't have a wife! I would like a wife!"

"*Ja ja,*" Nick say, "you gotta get a girlfriend before you get a wife. You got a girlfriend, Bobo? Or do you just use a hole in a coconut tree?"

Ja. That Nicky. Very funny.

That line, it takes five, six hours sometimes. Nick, you could see, he no used to it. He see the guy coming back *con dos jarras de* gasoline, and he told him, "I give you fifty dollars for the gas." But the guy no want it. Nick say, "Hundred dollars." The guy say, "*Que se moje los pies.*" *Tu sabes? El que quiere pescado que se moje los pies.* Like that.

By the time we got back, it was too dark to go driving. So, we tell Nick we would have a party. *Tu sabes,* not a real party, but we want *para celebrar* that he came to see us when things are really bad.

All we had to eat was Chef Boyardee, Spam, and rice. I told Nick I feel bad that's all we had to give him. "*Pero, cuando hay hambre, no hay pan duro.*"

He say, "I don't like that can stuff. What about *cabrito?*

That thing's just right there. Cabrito's f'ing delicious."

"*Ja.*" I laughed. But Bobo, he no laugh. Right away, he took Olga Tañón and hide her.

So we didn't have *cabrito,* but we had rum! And we had lamps all around the backyard, and Chuche started playing old records from her phone. Everything around was dark, black dark, and you see campfire and lights here and there, and you hear the coquis singing.

Nick, he got up and he grabbed Adriana to dance. And she had a few drinks and she was laughing. Everyone have a good time.

But then Bobo he come back from the woods, and maybe he had too much to drink. Blanca would know. Anyway, I think he want to dance, too, so he tried to get in with Adriana, but Nick no let him cut in, so Bobo took Nick's hands and started dancing with him! *Ja ja ja.* You should have seen Nick's face.

Ah, that was a nice party. We keep going until Chuche's battery die.

Anyway, the next day, Nick put the gas in the car and he go.

He came back in two hours, wet from his feet to his head. He say, "What happened to the f'ing bridge to Utuado?"

"*Inequívocamente la tormenta de la bruja María,*" I say.

He say he try to swim but that *corriente* was something else.

Blanca told him, "Why you want to go to Utuado? You crazy? It's the same as here. But they got less food and more mosquitoes." That's how she is.

"I need to get across the river," he say. "You know someone who got a boat?"

I told him there was my best friend Juan Pablo, but I

had not seen him since *la tormenta* when he went to go check on the boat.

Blanca, she cross herself when I say Juan Pablo, and then she say, "You should ask Bobo. His old teacher lives in Utuado, and he goes all the time to bring them food."

So, Nick go and talk to Bobo, but no joking this time. He say, "I have to get across."

And Bobo, say, "*Como no! Vamos!*"

So, they go and in two hours they come back, and Nick is wet again, his feet to his head. Bobo, *estaba todo seco.*

I say, "What happened?"

"This f'ing idiot," Nick say, "he takes me to a f'ing rope bridge, a rope bridge out a f'ing Indiana Jones movie, twenty feet about the f'ing water, three thin-for-nothing ropes, and he expects me to get across on that. So I tell him, I can't walk that f'ing thing. And you know what this motherf'er does? He picks me up like I'm a f'ing baby and starts carrying me across."

"So what happened?"

"What the f do you think happened? I'm not going to have a guy carry me like a baby. I fight him."

"He fell in the water. Splash!" Bobo say. *Ja ja ja.*

"I need a drink," Nick say. Then he tell Bobo, "One of these days, I'm going to find your f'ing goat and barbecue it good and eat it. After I f it to death."

Bobo, he no think that was funny. So he walked away, into the woods. Nick, he started drinking—he finished all the rum we had in the house—and he use the generator to start his phone and he played music, and Adriana came by from the line with five gallons of water, and she say she need a drink. And then those two got very close, and we left them alone.

Later, after all the lights were off, Adriana came to say goodnight to Blanca and me because she always did that. *Ella muy cariñosa.* She knock on the door, and we were under the mosquito net, almost sleeping. I could tell she had too much to drink. Blanca told her to come in, and she did and she sat on the floor and start crying.

Blanca say, "*Niña, tienes que tener cuida'o.* He's a nice guy, but you know how men are."

I didn't say nothing. I know to keep quiet. Women are always right, remember.

Adriana say, "He my only chance to get out. I got nothing. I lose everything."

And Blanca got up and she heat up some *leche evaporada* for her.

The next day, on the line for gasoline, I was with Nick, and someone tell him that if he drive up this mountain road and come down, the river is small and there's a little bridge right there and the road to take you to Utuado. That made Nick happy, so the next day he went out again in Adriana's car.

And when he came back, this time he was covered in mud. Blanca no let him in the house, and she gave him *un galón de agua* to clean himself outside.

He say, "I need workers. A couple of strong guys."

I told him, yeah, he could go to the gasoline line and ask people and they would help him. "*Cada cual sabe donde le aprieta el zapato.*"

"It can't just be just anybody. They can't be snitches," he say, and I say, "I'm sorry I'm too old, Felix is too skinny, Carlos is too old. But Bobo, Bobo is big and strong like ten men. Just ask Bobo."

So later he tell Bobo, "Adriana and I are going on an

adventure tomorrow, and we want you to come."

So, Bobo, he like adventure. He's like a kid. So he say he go.

The next day, I get up and they left, no good morning, see you later, have a nice day. Nothing. And someone came in the night and took my tools, my shovels, *un pico, tu sabes,* a pickaxe. *Ai yi yi.* Then it started to rain. *Un aguacero.* All day. Not like *la Bruja Maria, tu sabes,* but *lluvia* and wind and *lluvia.* '*chacho,* the last thing we need.

Night come and they no come back.

Then, three in the morning, I hear banging on the door. "BANG. BANG. BANG." There was Bobo, wet like a fish, and he had Adriana in his arms. He had mud all over. *Y sangre.*

I say, "Where is Nick? What happened?"

Blanca came out screaming. She got everyone awake. They got towels and bandages.

I look outside and I don't see the car. It's still raining, and the wind is still *gritando.*

"What happened?" I say. "Where is Nicky?"

Bobo, he was in shock, and Adriana was out, out, out. Blanca gave him some coffee. And little by little he talk.

Nick said they were going on an adventure. So he drive them to Utuado to *una finca abandona'o* up there in the mountains, I think the one that used to belong to your grandmother. Blanca knows. There's nothing there but a little house, used to be.

Bobo say they came to the house and because the mud *y la lluvia,* the house, it was hanging off the side of the cliff. And with the rain and the wind, it looked like it was going to fall any second.

So Nick say he needed this suitcase under the house. It

was under the floor, but the floor was dirt, and the dirt change to mud, and Bobo say he saw the suitcase right there, hanging under the house on the side of the cliff.

So, Nick he tell Bobo, he say, "Big boy, you go over the side and get that suitcase." He say that he would pay him money. But Bobo no care about money, one way or the other. Money mean nothing to him.

But then Adriana, she tell him, "Please do it. Bobo, you have to do it."

So Bobo, he look at her and he look at Nick and he say, "Okay."

They put a rope around him and hang him down. The rain was coming down and the mud, he say, "*Fue como un río.*" He say, "The mud was like chocolate, but it no taste like chocolate."

He reach and he reach and he grab the case.

"Pull me up!" he say. "Pull me up!"

And they pull him up, with the case. They get in the car, and Nick start to drive the car too fast. These roads here, they very small, and the mud was coming down all around. Bobo say he was scared.

Bobo say something hit the car or the car hit something. "*Como una bofeta' de Dios,*" he say. The car, it almost flew off the mountain, but Nick turn it and it spin and crash into the side, and mud and rocks came down. Down and down. Adriana, she had blood all over, and Bobo say Nick was stuck. The steering wheel move and pin him, and his legs got stuck under the steering wheel.

Nick scream at him, "You got to get me out here, you f'ing dummy."

Bobo say he can't drive, and the car was sideways.

Nick yell at him and say, "Yes, you can. You a f'ing ox.

Pull me out of here. Whatever it takes."

Bobo pull and pull, but Nick, he stay was stuck. Bobo him pulling.

"You f'ing this and this," Nick tell Bobo, "you gonna tear me in half."

Then Bobo, he got an idea. Now you know Bobo, *es buena gente.* He never hurt anybody. He just no understand.

He took the shovel—my shovel!—and he push it into Nick's legs, *asi y asi,* and chop them, *aqui,* in the meat, *tu sabes?* Then he pull Nick out. He pull the top and the legs stay. But, "He stop screaming," Bobo say.

Bobo pick up Adriana in his arms, and then took half of Nick and put him over his shoulder, and then he take the legs under his arm but they drop, and then Bobo tied them together and drag the legs in the mud.

But Bobo say, "I'm sorry, Tio Luis"—he call me "tio" even though he's Blanca's brother—he say, "It was too hard, *muy difícil, llevandolo*" down the mountain with the rain and with the mud. "Too much." He say he put Nick and his legs on the side of the road and covered him with banana leaves, and then he ran all the way back here with Adriana in his arms.

Ten miles in that *aguacero.*

Well, *puedes imaginar,* we had to call the ambulance and the police. There was a big mess and they went up there and they want to know what's going on and they try to find the body but with the rain and the mud they no find nothing. We didn't say what Bobo did because we no want him to get in trouble. Just in case.

La policia, they find the car and they say it empty. Except for *sangre.* They find a hundred-dollar bill in the trunk. The police come back, saying, "Who this money belong to?" and I say it must be Nick, he a big spender. They say, "You know he have a record? Do you know he was involved in drugs?"

I say, "I don't know about that, I no see him ten, fifteen years."

They say, "We check. He been coming to Puerto Rico every year, sometimes four, five times."

That was a surprise. "I don't know why he never visit. He's a good guy," I say.

Anyway, they took away the car. They never found your cousin, God have him in heaven. *La finca* is gone, it go off the mountain and into the trees and everything up there disappear.

Adriana, she decide to move to Florida. Everybody's going there now, everybody's leaving. It getting empty around here, *tu sabes?* Bobo, he move with her. She say he save her life. She say he her hero. Imagine.

Anyway, she got a nice house there, she say. She got a new car. They send us pictures all the time. They keep in touch. They send us a little something now and then, *tu sabes?* We got a new refrigerator, a TV set, air conditioner in every room. I got a new truck, but I still have to get on the line for gas sometimes.

They tell Blanca and me to come to Florida. "Move here." But we can't leave, no. This is home, *tu sabes?*

Yeah, it's still hard here. Still hard. We still have to use the generator. Doña Olga Tañón is still here, shitting all over the place. But, you see, everything going to be okay, *si Dios lo permite.* Right? And your Titi Blanca, she can make cake anytime now for you.

So, when are you coming to visit?

PAPA'S MANUSCRIPT
CHANTEL ACEVEDO

They stared at him as if they'd never seen him before, as if Javier Santiesteves was a lost tourist, trapped in the Finca Vigía museum after hours.

"Wh-What do you think?" Javier asked at last, breaking the spell, and then he was only Javier again, an intern from la Universidád de la Habana majoring in cognitive philology. He'd been hired to work on press releases for the museum, his knowledge of graphic design, and not philology, the reason for his hire. On his first day, Javier had said that he wanted to read Hemingway, and they'd laughed at him. Hadn't they all read Hemingway? But Javier replied, "No. I want to read Hemingway, the man, not his work." Only Patria Vargas, the director of the museum had had the courtesy to smile at Javier. When she walked by him, she had patted his shoulder tenderly, leaving a cool, throbbing spot Javier would think about at night.

Now, in his hands, Javier held a stack of yellowed paper. Typed and centered on the first page was a title, and beneath that, the name Ernest Hemingway. The pages trembled in Javier's grip, and he looked to Patria to steady himself. But Patria could not take her eyes off the thing he held in his hands. The tiny letters on the page were blurry in that way of old typewriters, so that looking upon the print Patria felt as if her eyes were going bad. She blinked hard.

"I found it behind the gazelle," he said. "Just plucked it out of the head's cavity."

There was a murmur in the room, a shudder that passed among the other curators, people trained to not touch anything except to brush it, lightly, with a feather duster. That was the first rule at Finca Vigía, Hemingway's home in San Francisco de Paula, Cuba, just outside of Havana. Do not touch anything except to clean it or mend it. Even the old wooden boat named Pilár, that iconic inspiration for *The Old Man and the Sea*, was an untouchable relic, housed in the yard underneath a metal carport. Once, a tree rat nested underneath Hemingway's fishing chair on the deck, and the curators had stepped onto the vessel on tiptoe. With every creak of wood, there were cries of "¡Ay!" and "Dios mío." The tree rat, whacked with a broom, ran out from under the seat, scurrying as fast as it could go. Its babies were gathered in a plastic bag and tossed into a nearby pond.

The house and its contents were kept precisely as if Hemingway had just been there, as if he might walk in at any moment, sweaty, flushed from his walk, and inspired. There were loose papers on his desk, lonesome leather sandals in the kitchen; the bathroom walls were covered in penciled notes where Hemingway had chronicled his weight and other details, such as "two hundred pounds after breakfast"; there were stuffed creatures everywhere, African animals mostly, their skins covering the floors, and the glass eyes of the trophies shining as if wet; there was the gamey scent of grass and blood everywhere in the house. The national heritage authorities descended on Finca Vigía every few years to check the plasterwork, to inspect the foundation, or to take stock of hurricane damage. They never counted the books in Hemingway's collection or noticed that the signed edition of *The Great Gatsby* was no longer among them, stolen long ago by either a tourist or another curator.

"Who gave you permission to take down the stuffed gazelle?" Ricardo Vargas asked Javier slowly, every word articulated in such a way that he did not sound Cuban, but perhaps Spanish or Argentinean. He was the associate director of the museum, and he answered only to Patria, who happened to be his wife. Ricardo was as large and bulky as Hemingway himself had been. On occasion, tourists thought he was an impersonator and asked to take pictures with him. Except for those moments when Ricardo smiled and puffed up his chest like a blue jay, he was a dour man, the precision of his speech an aftereffect of his troubles as a student at the University of Santiago de Cuba. His dissertation on Hemingway had barely passed through his Ph.D. committee after his advisor had relentlessly mocked Ricardo's English. Ricardo's pronunciation of names like "Hadley" and "Ashley" was deemed too harsh, too guttural, sounding very much like a cough when he said them. That was five years ago, during Cuba's "Special Period," those years after the Soviets pulled out for good, and people were eating banana peels and rags marinated in soy sauce and pretending it was meat. "What does proper elocution mean in a time like this?" Ricardo had roared at the professors on his committee. They'd given him the degree anyway and a recommendation for the museum post.

At Finca Vigía, Ricardo met Patria, at first falling in love with the thick braid she wore, a mammoth rope that hung down her back and brushed her hips as she walked, and later, with the way she handled Hemingway's things when dusting them—his books, his paperweights, and sundry artifacts of the great man's life—with fingers whose touch was feather light, the tips of them always cold, as if they were museum pieces too. Ricardo imagined her cool fingers on his chest every time he walked past her. He'd tug on her braid, and Patria would swivel to face him, her mouth a little crooked, then shake her head. Ricardo lisped the first time he spoke to her, saying "Buenaths" instead of "Buenas." She hadn't flinched, didn't seem to notice at all, but Ricardo was mortified anyway and bit his tongue angrily as if in repentance.

Ricardo kissed Patria for the first time in the kitchen, and she had marveled at the deftness of his mouth, the one that had given him so much trouble at school. They married in Hemingway's office, the extensive bookcases their altar, a pair of glistening elephant tusks on either side of the desk their attendants. That was five years ago. Now, whenever Patria's eyes rested on their wedding portrait, she felt a pang in her chest. How ill-considered, how like tourists, she thought, to marry in such a place.

At this instant, Ricardo's mouth was twisted in a snarl. "Who TOLD you to take the goddamned GAZELLE off the wall?" Ricardo yelled at Javier, and Javier lifted the manuscript up, as if it were a shield.

"Now wait," Javier said. "Stop a minute. I should have asked. I'm sorry. But isn't this bigger than a broken rule?" Ricardo was breathing hard, and Patria's cool hand on his did not calm him. The other two curators—both women, both named Carmen—were staring at Ricardo.

"We'll deal with the infraction later," Carmen Ríos said. She was a beautiful mulata with a long neck. Sometimes, tourists snapped pictures of her when they thought she wasn't looking. But Carmen Ríos knew what they were up to and would let her fingers relax wherever they rested, her hands perfect half-shells, posed, unnatural, and stunning.

"What a find. God, if it's real..." Carmen Balart said. Balart and Ríos were opposites in every way. They went by their last names at the museum, which both women seemed to like. Ríos, whose last name meant "rivers," resembled a ribbon of water when she walked, her movements liquid and seductive. Balart was portly, like a rum barrel, though her features were delicate and small. She was the kind of woman of whom it was said, "If she only lost some weight..." A third cousin of Fidel Castro's, and a fourth cousin of the Díaz-Balart senators in the United States, Carmen Balart was the only person on staff who could, and would, break the do-not-touch rule. During off hours, she could be found in Hemingway's own chair, a first edition of *The Sun Also Rises* in her hands. If she weren't such a devotee of Hemingway's, if she didn't know entire sections of *For Whom the Bell Tolls* by heart, and if she weren't a relative of el Comandante himself, Carmen Balart would have been dismissed. But as it stood, she'd caused no damage, and Patria liked the look on Balart's face as she read, feeling as if she'd stumbled upon the only happy person to ever exist on earth.

But now Javier Santiesteves had become the second person to break the rule, and his violation had yielded a treasure. The room was silent again. They were in the

Hemingway dining room. Pictures of Hemingway's sons were on the walls, encased in etched-glass frames. The boys held little kittens in many of the photos. The stuffed head of a lioness hung near the pictures, her golden fur drab and stiff. Patria hated this room, the kittens and the lioness. She hated the statue of the African pygmy in the corner. The room had no windows and was stifling. Sometimes, she thought she felt the hot breath of the lioness on her neck when she passed by it, then realized it was only the boiling airlessness of the room that caused the sensation.

"I wouldn't say it's as good as his other novels," Javier said. "Fascinating work, nevertheless. This book, more than any other, reveals Ernest's mind. It's definitely his work. Authentic."

"You mean you read it?" Ríos asked, and her eyes flared. Patria recognized the look. Accustomed to getting her way, Ríos was the portrait of a woman thwarted. She'd wanted to read the manuscript first. They all had. To be the discoverer of a lost Hemingway book! To feel for once what it must be like to be first, to explore and plunder the way the Spaniards did so long ago. Javier had put his fingers all over the pages, analyzed them, traversed the ridges and spills of Hemingway's mind. Looking around the room, Patria could see anger expanding like a balloon among the others. Ricardo, in particular, looked like he might die of an embolism.

"You fucking read it?" Ricardo said at last, breaking Javier's litany on the merits of the work.

Javier stopped short. He clutched the manuscript to his chest and cleared his throat. "Of course I read it. This belongs to the world of scholars now," and as he said it, his voice quivered. Patria could have killed him. It was a barb, she knew, at Ricardo, at his scholarly difficulties, and Ricardo reddened at once.

"We'll alert the authorities. Get in touch with the Minister of Culture. I'll call in the morning," Balart was saying. Patria was shaking. Ricardo gripped her hand in support, and she pulled it away and rubbed warmth into her fingers.

"No!" Javier said then, and his eyes were round and wild. For a moment, he looked like the lioness on the wall, and Patria felt her spine go rigid. "No, this is what we'll do," Javier said, running the back of his hand across his upper lip to clean the sweat there. "We'll study the book together, all of us. There's serious scholarship potential here. The papers we'll write! If they take the manuscript from us now..." Javier trailed off, his eyes resting on Balart, who had quietly taken out a notebook and was writing down minutes for the meeting.

"I'm not going to jail for your ambitions," Ríos said softly, while Balart scribbled a bit faster in a hard-to-read scrawl.

"Patria," Javier said, pleading. There was silence in the room then. Patria's name sounded foreign in her ears, though just the other night Javier had uttered it in a similar way, again and again, and she had felt as if he'd just named her, had just fashioned her into existence.

Patria felt as if she'd been sleeping with Javier for years, and as if they'd been talking about the virtues of the manuscript for just as long. The truth was, the situation was fairly new, only a month in the making, and now, before her fellow curators and husband, Patria felt exposed, as if the noon sun was upon her, and she imagined that they could not feel what she felt—a looseness in her limbs when her eyes fell on Javier, and a fierce, swelling possessiveness concerning Hemingway's book.

* * *

Javier had found the manuscript their first night together. She'd been busy closing up Finca Vigía for the afternoon, setting the bolts at each door and the locks on the windows with fierce swipes. She had caught Ricardo, just an hour earlier, giving a British woman a private tour of the estate, his hand on the small of her back. "Ju can seet on Hemingway's chair. Seet, seet. Ees comforble, no?" Patria heard him say as she peeked around the door. She watched him pocket a twenty-pound note while the tourist stroked the coarse hairs on his arm.

"I'm at the Hotel Nacional," the woman said, and Ricardo cocked his head a little, contemplating her. Patria emerged from the shadows and kicked the woman out then, in a flurry of Spanish and violent gesticulations that frightened the tourist. The woman had run out of the house, her flip-flops slapping the wood floors.

When Patria rounded on Ricardo, he held up the note sheepishly, the worn paper limp in his hand. "For that?" Patria yelled.

"It's a lot of money," Ricardo said, rolling the note into a tight tube and slipping it into his pocket.

"So what, you're taking lessons from the prostitutes on el Malecón?" Patria asked, the image of Ricardo's big hand on the tourist's back still in front of her. Ricardo said nothing, only looked at Patria with sad eyes. The other day, he'd mentioned, over dinner, the possibility of selling a first edition or two. Patria had felt something snap deep within her, a physical hurt, as if she'd broken something essential to her body. The room seemed to swirl around her, and when it stopped, she found herself considering

Ricardo's recommendation. What would a first edition of *Tender Is the Night* bring? Five hundred American dollars, easily. She caught herself then, yelled, "What are you thinking? ¡Loco!" and Ricardo changed the subject.

She thought of that moment again as she watched Ricardo fingering the rolled-up note tucked in his pocket, the tourist's gift. Ricardo and Patria stared at one another for a moment before he collected his things and left Finca Vigía. Patria listened for the engine of the car they'd earned through the state's lottery system, a 1978 Russian Lada, but heard nothing. The keys were on Hemingway's desk. Ricardo would walk in the dark so that Patria wouldn't have to.

That night, as she'd locked the doors and windows, she'd found Javier suddenly at her side. He coiled her braid around his arm so that it resembled a dark, moist snake. "He doesn't love Hemingway the way we do," Javier said. "I watched him with that woman. Letting her run her hands all over the desk."

Patria turned her head suddenly and found her braid trapped.

"Perdón," Javier said, and let go of her hair. "I'm just playing with you, you know. About Ricardo..."

"You're wrong," Patria said. "Ricardo is a devoted scholar. But times are hard. What is it people are saying nowadays, that we have to make do? Resolvér?"

"One shouldn't confuse art and politics," Javier said so grimly that Patria was reminded of the politicians on television with their set mouths and heavy-lidded eyes, their look both imperious and seductive.

"I wasn't aware you were so loyal to la patria," she said as she turned off lights around the house.

Javier said, playfully, "I have only one Patria," and she

knew he meant her and not the motherland, la patria, Cuba. "Don't say such things." She was thinking of the British woman, and her heart was pounding. "You have to be loyal to la patria, the only true patria," she said, sounding to herself like a young girl again, back in grammar school where they'd pledged to be like Che Guevara.

"Mm," he'd hummed and touched her hair again. He was no longer playing. "I'm sorry. I overheard what happened. Ricardo is an idiot to treat you that way," he said and kissed her neck. How did things move so quickly? Had Javier caught it like a scent, the knowledge that Patria was ripe for vengeance? They made a layer of clothes in the formal sitting room, atop a zebra skin that was thinning and shedding bristly black and white hairs.

Sometime around midnight, with the sound of tree rats scratching at the doorways, Javier said, sleepily, "There are rumors about this place, Finca Vigía. It's not like Hemingway's other home in Key West. This one has a basement, for one. So many letters down there, so many pages." Javier yawned, and on his breath Patria caught a whiff of something sweet, perhaps some guava, and her own mouth watered. "I'd like to transcribe all of it. The letters, the rough drafts, all of it, into a database. I'd know his mind then, Patria." Then Javier fell asleep, and Patria watched him a long time. She thought of her grandmother as she admired his youthful face, a woman named María Asela, who'd once warned her not to get involved with ambitious men. They are heartbreakers, she'd said, and Patria had laughed her counsel away then. Now, she was not so sure it was bad advice. Lying next to him, Patria felt a certain, deep anxiety, like the way one feels when standing someplace very high. Jumping was not a possibility, and yet, one could do it easily. All it took was a bit of impulse.

In the morning, Patria woke to find Javier already dressed, standing a few feet from where they'd slept, wiping his hands on his pants. There was a ridiculous smile on his face, and Patria felt a wave of nausea at the sight of him, so happy with his conquest.

Later, she'd understand that he'd been dusting his hands free of gazelle fur. How long had Javier Santiesteves been rummaging through Finca Vigía, like a child playing at treasure hunting? Javier had brought the manuscript to her during her lunch break, out on a second-floor balcony that was overtaken by bright pink bougainvillea. She had just taken a bite out of her buttered bread when Javier popped up before her. He ran his fingers along her jawline, and for one wild moment, Patria imagined what it would be like to continue the affair up there, hidden by the tangle of papery flowers.

"Mi Patria," he said, "look what I've found," and Javier thrust the brittle pages into her hands. There were about fifty pages, she guessed, and they'd been folded long ago into a thick square. The paper crackled in the wind. "It's an unfinished novel," Javier said, out of breath.

"Where?" Patria asked, though she could not hear herself. Suddenly, her ears felt stopped up, as if she were underwater.

Javier laughed. "Inside one of the trophies. A gazelle, I think. Way down in the snout. Why would you hide it? What a mystery you were!" Javier said, gazing up at the sky, as if he were conversing with Hemingway's ghost.

"We must turn it in to the heritage authorities," Patria told him, and Javier's laughter stopped all at once.

"They'll make me give it up."

"It will be studied, authenticated, Javier," and then, after a moment, Patria added, "You shouldn't have gone snooping without permission."

"They'll hold it hostage in Havana. The world will never see it," Javier said, snatching the manuscript from Patria's hands.

"Who's mixing art and politics now?" Patria asked, rising. She and Javier were the same height. She'd never noticed before.

"Fine," he said. "We'll read it first, though. Get our fill of it, agreed?" Javier held out his hand, and his face was set in mock seriousness. Patria took it, and he tugged her hard so that she fell against him, the manuscript trapped between their bodies. When he kissed her, Patria tasted guava again. She'd meant to ask him where he got it, as the sweet treat was rarely available, but she forgot soon enough.

The weeks that followed were both a misery and a source of elation for Patria. She and Javier would meet in the woods outside the museum and sit at the base of a great ceiba tree that was tangled up in liana vines. The ceiba, it was said, could not be struck by lightning and on the day they were caught out during a thunderstorm, Patria saw it to be true. Flashes of light would touch down here and there, but never where she and Javier sat close together, shielding the manuscript from rain. On drier days, they'd make sure to hang their clothes off high limbs, so that the tree rats would not scurry away with them for their nests. And always, they took time reading the manuscript together, working hard to translate the English, to untangle the sayings.

"'In a pickle.' What does that mean?" Javier would ask,

and Patria would, more often than not, have an answer.

"It's either, to be in trouble, or to have a stomachache. One of the two," she'd say, and Javier would laugh and kiss her again.

On their last afternoon together, Javier had held her so tightly that bruises formed on her back where he'd gripped her. "Que pasa?" she asked him, and he only smiled a little.

"I've got a handle on it now," Javier said, meaning the manuscript.

"What do you mean?" Her body ached, and she wanted desperately to arch her back, to push him off of her, but she didn't.

"How to get it out in the world."

"Javier, we have to turn it in. We shook hands and everything," Patria said. She found it hard to talk with his weight on her chest.

"'We shook hands'?" Javier repeated. "Ay, Patria, you love rules so much."

"What do you mean to do with Papa's manuscript?" she asked. They'd started referring to Hemingway as Papa now, the way the tourists did, because their affection for him had grown as they'd read his rough work, came to know his flaws, and understood him better for them.

"I don't know, I don't know," Javier said and finally sat up, grabbing at his hair. They wiped each other clean of twigs and dirt, then dressed in silence.

At home with Ricardo, Patria's joy would vanish. She'd had no right to be angry with him about the tourist. He'd done nothing, and she, Patria, had stepped into an affair so willingly. Ricardo would try to make small talk over dinner, but Patria was so distracted, both by Javier and the manuscript, that she did not hear her husband. One night,

Ricardo touched the back of Patria's thigh, and she jerked away. "To hell with it," Ricardo had said, and left their apartment.

It was a small moment, an involuntary jolt of her nerves that pulled away from Ricardo's touch. She considered her husband deeply that night, wondered why she'd agreed to marry him. It was his persistence, she thought. It was because no man had ever cooked for her before. It was because he blushed that first time he lisped in front of her, and she saw great tenderness in that. Patria's thoughts went on that way all night, so that when the sun rose, she'd decided to call things off with Javier.

She told him in their meeting spot by the ceiba tree. He'd swiped at his nose with the back of his hands, looked at her and nodded, nodded, as if he understood that things had to end between them. "Patria," he said only once and left the woods. Javier did not come back to work that day.

Late the next morning, Javier called the meeting in the dining room. "Patria," Javier was now pleading for the last time, and the other curators looked at Patria long and hard, having recognized a certain intimacy in his voice.

She wished for the power to read his mind now. What was he thinking? That the other curators would keep the manuscript's existence quiet? That Balart would finagle Javier some kind of position at the university?

"Leave it," Patria said, and Javier did, laying down the thick manuscript tenderly.

"And get out," Ricardo added. Patria winced. Something clicked in her throat, making it hard to swallow. Balart closed her notebook and put the cap back on her pen. Ríos sat back in her chair and crossed her legs, her left hand rubbing her shiny knee.

"I have only one Patria," Javier said before leaving Finca Vigía, and the others took it as a last-ditch effort to save face, to pledge loyalty to the state, to avoid any more scribbles in Balart's notebook.

Later that afternoon, the curators settled in the backyard of Finca Vigía, listening to the creaking of the fishing boat as a stiff breeze ran across its old deck. Closing her eyes for a moment, Patria imagined they were at sea and felt her body rocking to and fro of its own accord. They'd begun reading Papa's manuscript in the dying light of the day, Patria pretending to read the first page, one she already knew by heart, then passing it on to Ricardo, then to Ríos, who read quite slowly, her lovely lips moving in silence, and finally to an impatient Balart, who sighed as she read. Patria could not focus on the pages. Each scene was a reminder of Javier, of the ceiba tree, of the sweetness of his mouth. It was only when she reached page twenty-one that she noticed it. The paper was suddenly different. The yellow pages being passed around had the quality of age. They smelled musty. The bluish ink was smeared here and there. After page twenty-one, the paper was new, and there, at the top of the page, was a sentence that did not belong to the story they'd been reading. "For my patria" it began, then broke down into dummy text, that *lorem ipsum dolor sit amet* graphic designers used to substitute text. It broke down even further on page twenty-two, with the word *dolor* repeated for the rest of the manuscript, as if in apology of some kind.

Balart shot back into the house the moment they noticed the hoax. "I'm making a phone call," Balart said, pulling out a cell phone from her purse, an object that citizens were not legally allowed to own. Ríos kicked over one of the patio chairs, and it clanged loudly, startling a pair of crows in the distance.

"He's stolen the rest of it," Ricardo said.

Patria said, "There may not have been any more than this," and held up the first twenty pages. "The gazelle's head is not so big. A juvenile trick, that's all it was."

Ricardo covered his face with his hands. "Don't defend him," he said from behind his fat fingers, and it sounded to Patria like an accusation of infidelity.

Balart came outside again, still speaking on the cell phone. "Bueno," she said into it and then added, "Tomorrow at nine," before hanging up. She held out her hand, and Patria gave her the first twenty pages of the manuscript. "I've an appointment with the Minister of Culture. He's an old friend, you understand. He'll take it from there," Balart said, though she couldn't hide a smile. She would take the pages home, would read them again and again, Patria knew, would commit this work to memory. If it had to be one of us, Patria thought, I'm glad it's Balart, because she loves Papa so.

In the months that followed, countless Ministry representatives visited Finca Vigía. They'd interviewed them all in Hemingway's dining room, gathering information on Javier Santiesteves, who had disappeared. These were not aggressive meetings in the least, since Balart was always present, and she claimed the representatives as friends, all. Patria had told them what she knew about the young man, save for the night he'd appeared at her apartment, clutching a package.

The knock on the door had been whisper soft, but Patria heard it anyway. There was no need for quiet, as Ricardo had not come home. When she questioned him, Ricardo would say he was taking a walk along the seawall, that's all, but in the months since he'd begun his nighttime meanderings, he'd purchased a DVD player and a small freezer that was now stocked, regularly, with meat. What could Patria say? These were not bad things to own. The movies kept her company while Ricardo was gone. Anyway, she felt she deserved his absence. Still, it hurt to smell French perfume on him or to discover one afternoon, when they were showering together and trying to recapture some of the spark that had brought them to one another, a red bloom on one of his shoulder blades, in the shape of a small, insistent mouth.

Javier stepped into the apartment slowly, his eyes darting to the corners of the space, as if he expected Ricardo to emerge with a machete at any moment.

"We're alone," Patria had said. "Is that it?" she asked, pointing to the package.

"Sí," Javier said, and his voice cracked a bit, like a boy's.

"Why are you here?"

"I've missed you," he said. Patria knew then how a magnet felt. It took all her strength not to run into his arms.

"Why did you change the pages?" she asked.

"I thought we'd have to be honest then. 'For my patria,' you see? They were supposed to figure it out."

Patria couldn't help but laugh, and then, seeing the hurt on Javier's face, was sorry she did. "And then what, Javier? I get fired, divorced, and come back to you?"

"I've been in touch with someone in la Yuma, in New York, one of Maxwell Perkins' grandchildren," Javier said, ignoring Patria's question. He approached her slowly, and when he was close enough, he tugged on Patria's braid.

"Maxwell Perkins?"

"Papa's editor. Long dead." He was bouncing a bit now, drunk on adrenalin.

Watching him, Patria felt it again, that sensation that she was at sea. "I remember the name," she whispered.

"If I can get the manuscript to la Yuma, ay Diós, how rich we'll be!"

Patria shushed him then, afraid of the neighbors that slept only a few inches away. She pulled Javier further into the house and shut the front door.

"Excellent!" he said, and then, "Pack just a few things. We travel light." Already, Javier was tallying up the space, as if deciding for Patria what she might want to take with her.

Patria slumped onto the sofa in front of the television. The green light on the DVD player was throbbing, and Javier was tapping his foot in time to it. Patria was thinking of what to say next, but the words would not form into sentences. Instead, her thoughts were a muddle. Images of the stain on Ricardo's back, of the room at Finca Vigía loaded with books and dead things, of Javier's eyes shut tight as she watched him above her in the shade of the ceiba, and the sound of the sea in her ears assaulted her so that she could not think at all, except to say, "The manuscript is not yours to sell," which was true and which stopped Javier cold.

"And you didn't earn this DVD player through the state," Javier answered at once. His thinking, Patria noted, was not muddled at all. Javier and Ricardo were very much alike, Patria thought. She glanced at the package in his arms, and a great part of her wanted to leave with Javier, to give in to an urge the way she had before, but she thought tenderly of Ricardo, for all his flaws. There was her grandmother back in Oriente, and her brother and his children to attend to. There was the museum. Who would guard it if she left? There was Balart's black notebook. And Papa's manuscript, and a world that deserved to read it.

"Adios, Javier," she said then, stood from the sofa, and kissed his hairless cheek. So young, she thought.

Javier watched her for a long time. "So, that's it. This is how it ends?" he asked, and Patria nodded. His lip trembled a little. "Well," he said, "it's appropriate, I think. Papa would have liked an ending like this."

Patria managed a little laugh, but it sounded desperate in her ears. "He would have," she said. Javier drummed on the package with his fingers, sniffed once, twice, then left the apartment. Patria watched him go down the hall, her hands shaking terrifically, then shut the door.

That was a few weeks ago. Patria told no one about Javier's visit. Ricardo seemed to catch a whiff of something in the air of the apartment, standing there for a minute the morning after Javier left, then shrugged it off. As for Patria, she listened to the radio ceaselessly and read the *Granma* every day without fail, her fingertips blackened by ink, in hopes of learning about Javier's fate. Now, as she dusted Hemingway's things and led tourists through the house, snatching the rare first edition out of the hands of people here and there, she thought of Javier, fantasizing that he'd escaped, that the lost manuscript would be authenticated, and published, that Javier would find a way.

* * *

That November, three things happened of note: the first was Hurricane Paloma, a minor storm, which nevertheless damaged the left wing of Finca Vigía so badly that the museum had to shut down until after Christmas; the second was Ricardo's fling with an Australian ex-pat, a woman named Gloria, who fished for spiny lobster off the coast and brought Ricardo lunch on the weekends; the third was the radio report of a corpse washing up at Playa Larga, from which the authorities recovered only a digital watch and a swollen paperback copy of *A Moveable Feast*, Hemingway's Paris memoirs. Because she had not heard about him otherwise, Patria imagined that this was Javier, that he'd planned to escape by sea, that he'd been caught in Paloma's blustery weather and drowned in the torrent. Patria imagined, too, a patchwork quilt of yellow pages floating on the water momentarily before sinking. Such ambition, she thought, and clutched her chest.

THE SUNDOWNER

Jessica Laine

My name is Margarita O'Neill. I'm a twenty-five-year-old Latina from St. Paul with no romantic prospects, a minimum-wage job, and a creepy boss who makes love to my cleavage with his eyeballs. For the past three years, I've worked at the Barry Magnuson (or B.M.) detective agency near Pigs Eye Lake. I spend most of my time completing new client intake or creating background checks for employers. Once in a blue moon, I serve people with papers or do some surveillance on cheating spouses or *pendejos* trying to defraud insurance agencies with high-cost claims. It isn't my dream job, but my co-workers are cool. Most of us wish we didn't have to work for Barry Magnuson.

Barry pays us on time, which is the best thing I can say about him. As I review my to-do list, the scent of Drakkar Noir overpowers my nose.

"Aaatchooo!"

"Gesundheit," Barry whispers into my hair. For lunch, he eats either an onion or a tuna sandwich. At least, that's what his breath smells like.

"Thanks," I say, breathing through my mouth. "What's up?"

"I need to see you in my office."

Mierda. I don't need Barry trying to grope me before I've even finished my cup of coffee.

"Whatever you'd like to tell me, please feel free to say it right here."

"I don't think you want everyone to hear us converse," Barry says.

"Converse away."

"All right," he says. "Margarita, you're not meeting performance expectations. You'll need to attend another after-hours training session."

I know my performance is good—better than most. The last time I attended a so-called "after-hours" training session, Barry tried to stick his tiny hand down my blouse. Barry is a very short sixty-year-old man with bad breath and a walrus mustache. If I had another job opportunity, I'd bend his Vienna sausage–like fingers back until they broke.

"As I've told you before, my father is suffering from the effects of late-stage syphilis," I say. "My mother and I take turns caring for him, and my shift begins at 6 p.m. each night."

"Syphilis or not, I expect you to stay late tomorrow night," Barry says, his eyes never leaving my ample chest.

"Fine," I say.

My dad doesn't have syphilis. Even if he did, we wouldn't know about it. Dad left Mom for parts unknown about four years ago. After he left, I dropped out of the police academy because we couldn't afford the tuition. I held several jobs (selling rodeo tickets, holding a sign outside a fast-food place dressed as a chicken, and dancing in a cage at a nightclub) before landing this gig at B.M.

I live in my mother's garden apartment in the Hamline-Midway neighborhood to help pay the mortgage. As Dad used to say about Mom's cooking, my apartment is not too bad, but not too good, either. I've tried to make it homey with shade-loving plants and brightly colored cushions from Target, but I'm not fooling anyone. This is a subterranean dwelling, the kind only a creature of the night would dig.

My place is around the corner from a pub called The Sundowner. When Mom starts in on how I should be married with children, I can run out the door and have a drink in my hand in less than five minutes' time. Most of the regulars are like me, folks barely keeping their heads afloat in the river of middle class. It's not a flashy place, but as far as I'm concerned, The Sundowner is perfect: the drinks are reasonably priced, they offer live music on the weekends, and my best friend, Rhonda Gilliland, bartends there.

"Barry scheduled another after-hours meeting for tomorrow night," I say.

"I really hate that asshat. Why doesn't he grope someone his own age?"

"I don't know, but my work history is spotty. I need to stick it out at B.M. for a while. Otherwise, I'll never get a decent job."

"Never say never. Look at this." Rhonda waves at a bulletin board that is plastered in posters that say *Have You Seen Me?*

"The missing women? How can I help them?"

"Not them," Rhonda says. "This." She untacks a flier and hands it to me.

Looking for a new career? Have a private investigator's license? Call 651-555-1212.

I feel eyes on me. I stick the flier in my coat pocket and scan the room. A man stares at me from across the bar.

"Are you listening to me?" Rhonda asks. "What's up with you?"

"Nothing," I say.

Jake the bartender walks over and sets a pint in front of us. "Compliments of the gentleman." He nods toward the tall, dark stranger.

"Did you tell him I can't drink while I'm working?" Rhonda says.

"It's not for you," Jake says. "It's for Margarita."

When you're thin and gorgeous like Rhonda, you always think the drink is for you. The stranger nods at me. I nod back.

My annoyance with Rhonda evaporates when she says, "Why don't you go introduce yourself?"

"Why would I?"

"Because you think he's cute."

"How do you know?"

"You're blushing."

My face feels hot. Damned face.

Rhonda laughs. "See?"

"My life's already too complicated."

"Complicated in the wrong way," Rhonda says.

"Rhonda, are you on break?" a woman sitting at the bar asks.

"No."

"Then get me a fucking drink," the woman says.

"Nach í An Bhitseach í?" Rhonda whispers.

"What?"

"I said, 'Isn't she the bitch?' in Gaelic. She's a lot nicer when she isn't dieting." Rhonda wipes down the bar and heads toward the woman. "You should talk to that guy."

I check myself out in the bar mirror to ensure I don't have any salad bits between my teeth (I don't) and study my face: muddy-green eyes and olive skin framed by thick brown hair my mother likens to horsehair. I've been told I'm pretty but that my big mouth ruins my good looks.

Taking Rhonda's advice, I work up the courage to introduce myself to the stranger who bought me a pint, but when I glance at his stool, it's empty. *Mierda.*

I have two sets of clothes in my closet. One set is for the weekend when I want to enhance my natural assets. The other set of clothes reflects my desire to look as Oompa Loompa–like as possible during the work week. I have brown skin and brown hair, and most of my office clothes are brownish too.

This morning, I take no chances. I need this job and will look as hideous as possible to keep it. I don't wear any makeup and slap on a brown sweater with black vertical stripes. When I walk into the kitchen to eat breakfast, Mom makes the sign of the cross.

"*Hija*, what are you wearing? You look like an *espantapajaros*. A scarecrow. No man is going to want you looking like that!"

"Good." I slurp down my coffee and head out the door.

I don't want the after-hours training session to be a disaster. I don't want Barry to screw with me but—knowing Barry—

he probably will. Before I know it, it's five o'clock. My co-worker, Patty, hands me her travel-sized hair spray before she leaves.

"If he touches you, spray it in his face," Patty says.

"I will," I tell her.

When everyone is gone, Barry calls me into his office.

"Margarita," he says, gesturing at a chair in front of his desk. "Sit down, please. We're going to be here a while." He stands behind me and rubs my shoulders. "I hope we'll get to know each other better," he whispers in my ear. I can't be certain, but I think he had tuna for lunch today. I wonder what it's like to be a man, never being stared at, groped, or propositioned at work. It must be the bomb.

"Do you mind if I take off my sweater?" I say. "It's kind of warm in here."

"Of course," he says. "I want you to be as comfortable as possible."

I stand up and pull off my sweater.

I watch as Barry zooms in on my chest. "What's on your shirt?" he asks.

I borrowed a T-shirt from Rosemary, B.M.'s resident *kukufata*, or religious nut.

"Do you like it?" I ask him.

The graphic on the T-shirt looks like the ingredient panel on a box of cereal:

JESUS FACTS
Serving size: 1 Cup Serving per cup: 1 Life
Amount per serving:
Calories: 0   Calories from fat: 0
% of Daily Value:
Faithfulness: 100%

Self-Control: 100%
Forgiveness: 100%
Restoration: 100%

Barry looks like he's going to crap his pants.

"Well, it's *different*," he says, using the word Minnesotans use when they most want to damn someone or something.

"Yes, it is," I say. I pull a crucifix out of my pocket that I pilfered from Mom, the scary one that portrays Jesus bleeding and writhing in agony on the cross. I raise the crucifix over my head and walk toward him. "Tell me, Barry, have you accepted Jesus Christ into your life as your personal Lord and Savior?"

Barry realizes he's trapped in the corner of his office and can't escape my outstretched hands. I wave the crucifix in his face.

"I belong to the Church of the Open Door. We accept all sinners, even ones with peccadilloes as great as yours. I don't want your final resting place to be in Hades with Lucifer as your landlord. Join us."

Sweat streams down Barry's bald head as I move closer to him, and his eyes dart toward the door behind me. "Cleanse yourself! Redeem yourself!" I shout. And then I step on his foot and feel a satisfying crunch.

Mom is a daytime shift supervisor at a taco shell factory. Traditionally, Peruvians don't eat tacos, but here in Minnesota everyone eats tacos, so no biggie. She gets off work at 4 p.m., and dinner is usually ready by the time I get home from the detective agency. Tonight, the kitchen lights are dimmed, and the radio is off.

"Mom?" I call out.

No answer.

I head up the stairs and knock on her bedroom door.

"Can I come in?"

The bedroom is a mess. Drawers have been ripped open. Piles of clothes cover the floor. The television is blaring. Mom is curled up on her bed, crying.

"Mom, what's going on?"

She turns toward me. For the first time, I think she looks her age, maybe older.

"I've been let go," she says.

"From work?"

She nods.

"Wow."

"That's all you can say? 'Wow'?"

"Sorry, I don't know what to say."

Truth. I wasn't ready for Mom to tell me she's been let go. Sweet Jesus. Now is not the time to tell her I've been fired. I feel like I'm in one of Mom's telenovelas. A bad one.

I need a drink.

"I'm going out for a while."

"*Ten cuidado.*" Be careful, Mom says. "They found one of those missing women."

"Where?"

"In the Mississippi River. The police are investigating."

"That's terrible."

"The world's a terrible place," Mom says. "Take your pepper spray."

* * *

It's nine o'clock on a weeknight. You'd think The Sundowner would be quiet, but it's not. There's a band playing Irish music. Some people are dancing. Some people are watching the people dancing. A few guys are looking at me. They have that glassy-eyed look men get when they've been drinking. I don't look back.

I sit on a bar stool and kill time by admiring the interior of the pub. The walls are painted a dark forest green and decorated with prints by local artists. A large oak bar with a mirror dominates one side of the pub.

"Penny for your thoughts?" Jake the bartender sets a pint down in front of me.

What would Jake say if told him I pretended to be a *kukufata*/religious nut at work and got fired?

"I wouldn't even know where to start," I say.

"Fair enough," he says. "Catch you later."

When the crowd thins, Rhonda stops by. "Did you hear they found the body of one of those missing women?" she says.

"Yeah, I heard."

"Sad."

"Sad," I agree.

"What happened with the handsome stranger?"

"From last night?" I say. "Oh, nothing."

"Nothing?"

"He left before I could introduce myself."

"*Chica.*" She shakes her head. "How did your training session go?"

"I got fired." I tell her the whole story.

"Worst-case scenario, Sex World is hiring. You have big boobs. You could get a job there," she says.

"Come on, be serious."

Rhonda laughs. "What about that flier I gave you?"

"Hey Rhonda, can you help me out?" Jake says.

"Sure thing." Rhonda walks away.

I reach into my coat pocket and pull out a crumpled wad of paper.

Looking for a new career? Have a private investigator's license? Call 651-555-1212.

The next day, I drive to an older office building down by the Mississippi. A hand-written sign that says "Interviews Here" has been taped to an office door that looks like it's been kicked in one time too many. The interior has been painted an unappealing shade of blue. The furniture is cheap, and there are no pictures on the walls. It looks like a space that could be cleared out quickly. I'm about to take off when a young woman with a pixie haircut and a military bearing opens the door to the inner office.

"Margarita? I'm Robin St. Clare." She looks at her Apple watch. "Right on time. Punctuality. I like it. Come on in."

Once we're settled, she asks me a couple of general questions. We talk about the police academy and why I had to leave and my work at the private detective agency and then she offers me the job. She won't tell me about the position until I sign a contract of employment.

"Why would I sign a contract without knowing what the job entails?" I say.

Robin hands me a piece of paper. "Here's your starting salary."

The salary is more than I've ever made. It's more than I thought I'd ever make.

"Most people in your situation don't hesitate to sign,"

she says.

What the hell does Robin St. Clare know about my situation? I picture Mom lying in a crumpled heap on her bed.

"I need to think about it," I say.

Robin's smile slides off her face. Her doe eyes—so black they're almost colorless—stare at me. She doesn't seem as friendly when she's not getting her way.

"Better think fast," she says.

I skim the employment contract, which says the company assumes no liability in the event of death or dismemberment. While the language is disturbing, let's face it—opportunity isn't exactly knocking down my door. I sign my name on the dotted line.

"Who do I work for?"

"An employer who would prefer to remain anonymous."

"What's the deal?"

"What do you mean?"

"What's the catch?"

Robin laughs. "I like you, Margarita. You're sharp. We hunt down criminals."

"And?"

"They're monsters."

Obviously, my new employer *es loca*, but her check clears, so I shelve my doubts.

Tonight, I'm at The Sundowner in a professional capacity. I may not be every man's cup of tea, but a pretty face goes a long way at. I spend most of the night keeping the sharks at bay, especially the *mañosos* with grabby hands. I don't appreciate men who try to pinch an inch.

It's almost midnight. The person in the photo that my

employer, Robin St. Clare, gave me hasn't shown up yet. While I'm debating what to do, a traveling businessman from Cleveland asks me to slow dance. I hesitate because I'm on the clock, but it's been a long time since I've danced with someone. I miss the smell of a man, the feeling of his arms around me, so I accept.

Bad idea. The salesman pins me against the railing of the dance floor with his crotch. I'm struggling to free myself when someone picks him up and hurls him out the front door.

"Are you all right?" My savior has an accent, the kind that makes panties drop.

"Yeah," I say, a little dazed. "Thank you. That guy was a jack hat. I'm Margarita."

"I'm Killian," he says. "Can I buy you a drink?"

The Sundowner attracts traveling businessmen, career drinkers, and women who've settled for less. One of the regulars, a thin woman dressed like a librarian in a cardigan and pearls, seems to be giving us the evil eye. Killian doesn't appear to notice.

Sipping my beer, I study Killian. He threw the salesman from Cleveland out the door like he was throwing out the trash, and he hasn't even broken a sweat. He's thinner than my usual type but has an interesting look. Curly black hair and light blue eyes. A nose that looks like it's been broken a few times perched over a full, red mouth. Possibly the palest skin I've ever seen. Something about him seems familiar.

Eventually, I realize he's the man in the photograph that's burning a hole in my purse.

Recently, a handful of women have gone missing from The Sundowner. In a strange coincidence, the women had lost a significant amount of weight in the weeks leading up to their disappearances. Robin St. Clare thinks the man in the photograph—Killian—may have a connection to the missing women.

"This isn't the first drink I've bought you," he says.

"It's not?"

"No."

"Was that you the other night?"

He nods. "Do you want to get out of here?"

The gun in my purse gives me the courage to say "Yes."

"Your place or mine?" he asks.

Mom is probably watching television right now, blaring a *telenovela* in the living room above my garden apartment. I stifle a shudder.

"Yours," I say. "Where do you live?"

"Not far from here." Killian grabs my hand and we leave.

His apartment isn't super-fancy, but it's neat and clean. It doesn't *feel* like the home of a serial killer. Nevertheless, I follow my employer's instructions.

"Where's the bathroom?" I ask.

Standing over the bathroom sink, I text Robin St. Clare. *Suspect located. Interviewing now.*

I rejoin Killian in the living room. "Where are you from originally?" I ask.

"Ireland."

"How did you end up here?"

"By chance."

"How do you like it?"

"It's fine. A little cold. Less rainy than Ireland."

"What do you do?"

"This and that."

"Do you go to The Sundowner a lot? I don't think I've seen you before."

"Just a handful of times over the past few weeks."

The past few weeks. When those women went missing.

"Do you do this often?"

"What?"

"Pick up women?"

"Why?"

"Just wondering."

"Is this an interrogation?"

"No."

"Feels like one."

"It's not."

"Good," he says. "Want a tour of my apartment?"

I don't answer.

"Come on." He flashes me a grin. "Promise I won't bite."

"Okay," I say.

It's a short tour. He shows me the kitchen and living room, and then we end up in the bedroom. Killian pats the bed.

"Care to join me?" he asks.

"I don't know," I say. Sleeping with a suspect, especially one who might be a serial killer, is generally frowned upon by my employer.

"Give me a chance," he says. "I promise you won't regret it."

Under normal circumstances I would've been out the door, but something about Killian makes me hesitate. Maybe it's the way he said I wouldn't regret staying. I place my purse on the dresser.

I wonder if Killian is going to try and kill me?

Even if he is, I feel like I'll die satisfied.

And I haven't been satisfied, not for a *long* time.

I lie on the bed naked, trying to relax. I like my curves, but I'm self-conscious. I cover myself with my hands.

"I want to see you," Killian says.

He brushes my hands aside and kisses his way down to my stomach. The rest is a blur. He does *something* but honestly, I don't know what. All I know is I call out his name again and again.

Early the next morning, I slink out of Killian's place while he sleeps. Today, the air smells fresher, colors look brighter, and people seem nicer—except Mom.

"*¿Qué te pasa, hija?*" she asks.

I picture Killian naked. "Nothing. Why?"

"*No te ves bien,*" she says. "You don't look good. Are you losing weight? You should eat something."

When your mother is Peruvian, you can never be fine—you're either too fat or too thin. Now that Mom mentions it, my jeans feel loose. When I bought them, they were tight as hell. Strange.

"I'm not hungry," I tell her. "I'm going out."

"*¿Otra vez?*"

"Yes, again."

"When will you be home?"

"Don't wait up."

I sit in The Sundowner, waiting for Killian to show. The thin lady who looks like a librarian stares daggers at me from the end of the bar.

"Hello," someone whispers in my ear. Killian. We don't stick around. Instead, we race back to his apartment.

In the morning, I ask him, "Who's the skinny lady? The one who hangs out at The Sundowner?"

"Which lady?"

"The one who looks like a librarian."

"Oh, Norma," he says. "She is a librarian."

"What's her deal?"

Killian looks uncomfortable. "We were an item once. It's over now."

"Is it?"

"For me, it is," he says. "Are you ready for round two?"

While I'm getting dressed, Killian says, "I have to work tonight."

Disappointment races through me. "Okay," I say.

"Can I meet you at your place later?" he asks.

I smile. "Sure."

Last night, another woman disappeared from The Sundowner. It happened while I was with Killian. At first, I'm thrilled Killian isn't a killer, but then I realize he could have a partner. Some killers work as a team. Or the killer could be someone else entirely. In any case, I need to head back to The Sundowner to investigate.

It's a quiet night at the pub. As Rhonda pours me a drink, I catch sight of myself in the mirror. My jeans are baggier than before. Alarm bells ring. Didn't those women lose weight in the weeks before they disappeared? And my weight loss didn't begin until I met Killian. I look at my watch. Killian will be at my place soon. I make sure the gun in my purse is loaded—just in case.

As I slide the key into the lock, my front door swings open.

"Sit down," Norma the librarian says, pointing at the couch, "or I'll kill him." She's holding a wooden stake at Killian's throat. I notice his hands are tied behind his back. Above us, Mom's telenovela drowns out the noise in my apartment. She'll never hear anything until it's too late.

"What's going on?" I say.

"Ha!" Norma laughs. "I want to be thinner, but this asshole won't help me."

"What do you mean, he won't help you?"

"You're not very bright, are you?" Norma says. "You don't even know what your new boyfriend really *is*."

I consider my rapid weight loss. Killian—so thin when we met—has filled out. More than a normal person could over the course of a few days.

"He's a fat-sucking vampire, you dumb bitch!" Norma yells.

"Norma," Killian says, not meeting my gaze, "if I suck out any more of your fat, you'll die."

"That's not true!" Norma says. "You got tired of me, and now you're sucking the fat out of other women. You know what, Killian? You're a fat-sucking man-whore, and I hate you! You ruined my life!"

I glance at my purse, which lies within arm's reach. "What happened to the other women, Norma?" I ask.

"I killed them," she says. "And now I'm going to kill *you*."

Norma runs toward me with the stake raised high

above her head. I grab the gun out of my purse and shoot her point-blank. She drops with a loud thump. I hear Mom's footsteps thundering above us as she crosses the living room to switch off the television.

"*¿Margarita, qué pasa?*" Mom yells through the vent. "*Todo bien?*"

"Fine," I yell back. "I dropped a pan."

"*Eres un caballo,*" Mom says. "You're so clumsy, *hija.* You worry me." She turns the television back on, full blast.

I untie Killian. "You should go," I say.

"What about Norma?" he asks.

"I'll take care of her."

Killian vanishes into the night.

Robin St. Clare isn't pleased when I call her to say Norma the librarian/serial killer is lying dead in my apartment, but she agrees to send over a clean-up crew.

"Where's the original suspect? Killian?" she asks.

"Why?"

"The department will want to bring him in," she says. "Conduct research on him."

I almost drop the phone.

"Margarita, are you still there?"

"Yes."

"You know he's not human, right?"

"Right."

Killian may not be human, but he's no monster. Not like Norma. Or my employer, Robin St. Clare.

"You have twenty-four hours to find him," she says.

* * *

I walk over to Killian's place.

"You need to leave," I say. "Now."

He kisses me. "Come with me."

I shake my head. "You can't feed from only me. You need sustenance from other women, and I'm a jealous Latina. I don't want to end up like Norma."

Killian wraps me in a tight embrace.

"I'll miss you," he whispers into my hair.

"I'll miss you, too," I say. "Go."

"Margarita?"

"Yes?"

"I'll never forget you," he says.

We kiss again.

"Now go," I say.

And I watch as he walks out of my life.

Robin St. Clare fires me. Life returns to normal. Mom asks me when I'm going to meet a nice man. I tell her I met a nice man.

Mom rolls her eyes. "*Hija*, that wasn't a nice man," she says. "That was a *pishtaco*, a fat-sucking vampire."

"You knew?"

"*Por supuesto*," she says. "You think you're the only one who's ever been chased by a *pishtaco*?"

My mother? And a *pishtaco*?

"Besides, they like the *gorditas* like you," she says.

"Now I'm too fat again?"

"Fatter is better," Mom says. "You looked like *un esqueleto*—a skeleton—when you were too skinny."

* * *

A certified letter arrives, postmarked from Ireland. My heart pounds as I tear open the bulky envelope. Inside is a deed of ownership to The Sundowner and a note:

I'll never forget you.—K.

I move out of my mother's house and buy Killian's old apartment. I like living there. The ghost of his scent, a mixture of oak and whiskey, still lingers in the bedroom. Someday, I'd like to meet someone, but life is busy. I'm not holding my breath.

My days at The Sundowner are spent meeting with vendors, booking musical acts, and scheduling work shifts. I promote Rhonda to general manager. Together, we revamp the menu. I add two drinks: margaritas (of course) and our bestseller, The Pishtaco. When people ask me how I came up with the name of our most popular drink, I tell them they wouldn't believe me.

LA BACA
CHRISTOPHER NOVAS

Eddy's contorted, damaged face was burned into Cristina's mind, his body suspended on the Puente Juan Bosch, swaying with the morning wind. She climbed the stairs to the central police station for the fourth time that week. On the second floor was the bullpen, where the detectives sat going over paperwork, eating breakfast sandwiches while drinking coffee. The receptionist gave her an exasperated look and sighed.

"Mrs. Rodriguez, I've told you again and again. When the detectives have found something, they will call you. Please, go home and wait," he said.

"I have been waiting. And waiting and waiting. My husband has been dead for four weeks! He was an honest, hardworking man, not a goddamn dealer. Are you even trying to find who killed him?"

"I'm going to have to ask you to calm down, or you'll be escorted out of the building, Mrs. Rodriguez," the receptionist said, taking a sip of his coffee.

None of the detectives had spared a glance to her outburst.

"Malditos!" Cristina screamed as she slammed her hands on the desk before she left.

She tried to keep up with her life. See friends, go to work at the hair salon, go to the gym, but the quiet was always there when she settled in back home. The cold, empty side of the bed greeted her every morning. On the nights when she couldn't sleep, during the witching hours, she'd walk the streets of her barrio. Cristina watched people drink Presidente beer and listen to bachata or salsa pulse through upgraded car speakers, their rhythms and vocals echoing up and down along main roads and throughout the surrounding neighborhood. Prostitutes lined up outside of their homes with the dim light of the streetlamps accentuating their bodies, their shadows hugging the doorways. Cars parked along the street across the makeshift brothels, and men shuffled in and out throughout the long night. Cristina sat across the street, watching the exchanges until the sunrise.

Light pierced through the bruised sky. The streets glittered with broken glass, stars on the cracked gravel. Cristina got up from her perch as the stray cats and dogs awoke from their slumber and went in search of food, water, or a loving hand. Smoke and the putrid stench of burning garbage wafted throughout the neighborhood. Cristina walked past a colorful home, even by Dominican standards. Patterns of cream-colored branches and leaves accented the light blue walls, and bronze bars lined the windows and doors. A doña, tanned with a buzz-cut salt and peppered hair, sat outside in her rocking chair, holding a cup of steaming coffee in the already warm morning. She wore an oversized muumuu, the skin on her upper arms sagging as if she had recently lost weight.

"Buenos dias, señorita. I've been watching you sitting there all night. Was wondering when you'd get bored and leave," said the doña as she took a sip of her coffee.

"Why?" Cristina asked with a raspy, tired voice.

"Wondering why you're so fascinated by the meretrizes," the doña said.

She took a moment to think, then Cristina said, "I suppose I liked the power. The right look across a dark room, a hand on a shoulder, the way words hang out of our mouths like rainwater for the thirsty."

The doña took another sip of her coffee, then bent and put her cup down on the tiled floor. She gave Cristina a long look, then said, "Have you ever had your cards read to you?"

"What?"

"Your cards, mija. You'll understand if you come in. You've had a long night. Come in, have some coffee, relax for a bit."

The doña's name was Dolores Fuentes. She lived in El Malecon alone, save for her cats. Domestic disputes, cheating boyfriends or husbands, the health of their child or grandchild, everyone came to Dolores with their qualms. She was known as la bruja del barrio, the neighborhood witch. Cristina had heard the stories, rumors floating past her ears about the mysterious bruja, but she never investigated for herself. Dolores prepared coffee in a steel, single-serve kettle as Cristina waited in the living room. Unlike the boisterous color of the exterior, the interior of Dolores' home was sparse. Clean, white walls, worn oak furniture with a hint of polish, a few abstract paintings from Dominican artists hung on the walls—a coconut vendor on the beach, a farmhand at work, among others.

In front of one of these paintings was an object wrapped in cloth. Its tip exited the cloth. It looked like the tooth of an animal, Cristina thought. She walked up and reached her hand out to it. "Don't touch that!" Dolores said louder than she intended. Cristina immediately pulled her hand back. "I'm sorry that's, that's a family heirloom. I don't like when people try to touch it," Dolores said. Dolores' hands were slightly shaking as she handed Cristina her a cup of coffee.

"No, no, I should apologize. I should be more respectful in your home," Cristina said, accepting the cup.

They sat on an old couch that was covered completely in plastic. In front of Cristina was a deck of cards, brown, with silver framing a geometric pattern of a cube. Cristina had friends who had had their cards read to them. The way the cards fell, their images upright or upside down spelled out stories of love, tragedy, success.

"First, you must know that my brujeria mainly comes from God," Dolores said as she shuffled the deck, then cut it in half, placing the bottom half on top. Dolores proceeded to take five cards at random from the deck and laid them face up for Cristina to see—The Lovers, Death, Five of Cups, Six of Pentacles, and The Empress. Dolores examined the cards she set out, scrunching her face as she swept her eyes left to right.

"Ay mija," Dolores let out. "Something...something terrible has happened to you, verdad?"

Cristina kept her eyes between The Lovers and Death.

She wiped away a tear that rolled down her cheek, and she said, "My husband...he was murdered almost a month ago." Dolores gave her a quick hug and words of condolences. Afterward, they finished their coffee, and Cristina went to the door. Dolores put her hand on her shoulder, stopping her before she exited.

"What you talked about earlier, ese poder. What would you use it for?" Dolores asked.

"Venganza," Cristina said.

"I think I can help you with that," Dolores said, her teeth glinting in a scythe-like smile.

Dolores had explained that the tarot wasn't real magic, more like God's hands showing you the possibilities of your life. Dolores would teach her magic, real magic. Potions to make people speak the truth, undetectable poisons, spells to crush someone's psyche. Dolores told Cristina stories of the men she had conquered in life, some she had to push away with magia, though that was rare. A month into her training, Cristina received a pearl pendant and a tube of lipstick from Dolores.

"The pendant is from my mother and her mother. It's kept us all safe throughout the years, and I want you to have it. I'm sure it'll bring you luck, mija. As for the lipstick, well, just open it and you'll see," Dolores said.

Cristina did as she was told and pulled on the head of the tube. A two-inch blade appeared where the lipstick should've been. The steel shined in the living room light.

"Just in case a motherfucker tries something," Dolores said.

Two more months passed; the anger and grief festered

and bubbled over in her lonelier moments. She had stopped taking phone calls from family and friends. The charade of keeping herself glued together after Eddy's murder had exhausted all her energy for social norms. Empty bottles of Brugal lined the dining room table in Cristina's home. The only regularity of her life was contained in work and visiting Dolores. One night, after her shift at the hair salon, she found Julio, one of Eddy's closest friends, waiting outside her home.

"Julio! What are you doing here?" Cristina squealed excitedly, squeezing his slightly pudgy yet muscular body.

"It's nice to see you too, Chichi." Julio hugged her tightly in return. "Sorry I haven't been around. Can we talk inside?"

"Claro, claro, come in."

Julio entered Cristina's home and sat in one of the two rocking chairs on the small deck. Cristina went to the kitchen and handed him a cup of Rica orange juice, filled to the brim with ice as he rocked gently near the open window, taking in the breeze.

He thanked her, downed the juice, and began crunching on ice as Cristina sat on the rocking chair opposite him. "I'm piecing together what happened with Eddy," he said.

Cristina paused, took in a deep breath, got up, and started pacing.

"I've been talking to the low-level dealers around here, taking them out to lunch, greasing their palms, checking out who Eddy might've messed with. He found some perico near the Ozama River and was looking for someone to sell it to," Julio continued, crushing the ice cubes between his teeth. "He just wanted the money to help you. To get you both out of here."

Cristina stopped pacing. "And what's wrong with living here, decently?" Cristina said, stretching her arms around the room. "I'd been saving for months from my tips and salario from the salon. I wanted us to leave too. He had to get the easy money. Had to be impatient. Had to go get himself—" Cristina's words trailed off.

She took a breath and continued, "Finally, someone knows something. I haven't heard from those puto cops for over two weeks."

"Maldito vagos, lazy fuckers, can't trust them. They've wiped their hands of it," Julio said.

"Fuck the cops. If you're going to talk to more dealers, I'm coming too," Cristina said.

Julio started, "It may not be safe—"

"I don't give a fuck, Julio. If they know anything, I need to know," Cristina said.

"You don't know these people, Chichi. They're the type to fuck you up if you say the wrong thing," Julio said with a concerned voice.

"You've been doing just fine hanging with them, not even being in their world. Besides, I don't need your machismo bullshit, Julio. I can take care of myself."

"Okay...okay. Just stay close to me, please."

Cristina and Julio took a cab and headed to Feb. 27, just over Puente Juan Bosch. The sun-beaten buildings had been stripped of their color, the gray slashes of concrete peering through shades of yellow, red, and green. Children played in the evening sun, their shadows dancing along the walls. Construction was ever ongoing, with cinnamon-colored dirt and rock formed into neat piles of destruction near sidewalks, cordoned off with yellow tape. The day's food stalls were slowly being moved away to make room for the chimichurri trucks and night stalls.

During the cab ride, Julio quietly explained that Gabriel was the leader of the dealers around the area. Their cab stopped near the entrance of a dead-end street.

"Senores, no voy mas. Too many bad things happen around here," said the cabbie.

They paid the man 100 pesos and exited the cab. They walked down the wide street like antelopes around lions. The children stopped and gawked at them for a few seconds before continuing their hopscotch. People perched on the barred windowsills, living gargoyles of the neighborhood, watched them go by.

"So, Gabriel lives in this dump?" Cristina asked.

"He's all right for a small-time dealer, unless you try to sell without his permission. He'll cut off your hand for that," Julio said matter-of-factly.

They stopped at a watermelon-green building and climbed the steps to the third floor. There, they went down the small corridor lined with barred, open windows all along its right side. Julio knocked on a nondescript door in the middle of the hallway. Its bronze plaque, numbered 12, was painted over hastily to cover up its rust. A small hatch opened in the center of the door.

"¿Con quién deseas hablar?" asked the voice beyond the door.

"Gabriel. Tell him it's Julio, and I've brought a friend," Julio said in a calm voice.

The door swung open, and the smell of marijuana and beer filled the tiny hallway. When they stepped inside the dark, smoky room, Cristina saw that the man was holding a Glock 19 against the doorframe with his finger on the trigger. Cristina instinctively put her hand, slowly, in her right pocket where she kept the concealed knife.

"Can't be too careful," the doorman said with a small smile.

He led them into the kitchen, where a dark, tanned man sat on the counter eating a plate of arroz con habichuela with stewed chicken.

"Primo! Who's the beautiful lady you brought with you today?" Gabriel said as he set down his plate, gave Julio a quick hug, and eyed Cristina behind his back.

"Gabriel, Cristina."

Gabriel planted a kiss on the back of her hand.

"Nice to meet you too," Cristina said with a smile. She discreetly wiped the back of her hand on her jean leg, away from Gabriel's view. The doorman behind her gave a small chuckle.

"I know you're not here to buy, and you're definitely not here for a social visit. So, what do you two want?" Gabriel said, waving his used fork between them.

"Informacion," said Cristina

"About?"

"Your competition. Not the pendejos you'd shit-talk on the streets. Not the boys who sell dirt weed in the dark alleys. Your real competition—the one who'll sell perico like it's powder for a baby's ass," said Cristina.

"Why would you want something like that, hermosa?"

Cristina took out a wad of bills from her back pocket and threw it on the counter. It had been more than half of her savings thus far, but now that Eddy was gone, what was the point in keeping it? Better use it here and get something out of it, she thought.

"There's about eight thousand there. What's his name, and where does he usually party at?"

"You motherfuckers aren't playing around, huh?" Gabriel said as he flipped through the stack. "What's stopping me from jacking your shit and telling my man to give you a little wear and tear on the way out?"

Julio was about to start saying something, but Cristina interrupted him.

"You wanna live like this forever? Here, in a dying building with only one way out?" Cristina nodded to the open window behind Gabriel. "You want this motherfucker dead or not?"

Ricardo Aguilas partied at a nightclub called Paradise on the Malecon, Friday and Saturday nights. He always arrived around 11 p.m. with an entourage of about five men—his bodyguards and two new pieces of arm candy for the night, never the same pair of women on any given weekend.

Cristina and Julio scoped out Paradise the night before. Inside, the music pulsed in time with the strobe lights changing colors; marble tables lined the corners; sand was thrown about the floor; and seagulls, coconuts, and mini palm trees were painted on the walls. The patrons were a mix of locals and people coming in from all over the city. Even on a Thursday night, it was decently packed. Cristina and Julio had a few drinks, then left.

The next day, with the morning sun looming overhead, Cristina knocked on Dolores' door. Dolores led her to the living room, fetched her a cup of coffee from the kitchen, and set it on the table.

"I found him," Cristina said, her hand shaking as she

lifted the cup to her lips.

"Senti que si, mija. Do you feel ready?" Dolores asked.

"Bien. I have one last thing I want to give you, and you must promise me you'll be careful with it," Dolores said, getting up and going to the clothed object that sat in front one of her paintings. "Never touch it directly. Leave it close to him, and let the magic run its course," Dolores said.

Cristina carefully took the clothed object.

The line to get into Paradise went up the block as Cristina walked down the street in her skin-tight red dress and black heels. The men in line stared at her, transfixed by the glow of her brown skin, down to where the pearl pendant hung between her breasts. She reached the security guards and slipped a few hundred pesos from her black purse and into one of the guard's hands before walking into the glow of Paradise. Jose Manuel Calderon's singing bled out into the streets. She spotted Julio eyeing her at one of the reserved tables they paid for the night before but moved toward the VIP section where she saw Ricardo Aguilas with his new set of women for the night. She asked the bartender for a vodka martini, stirred, with two olives. Drink in hand, she stepped toward the group of three, but one of Ricardo's bodyguards stopped her midway. Ricardo looked up at her with eyes glazed, half drunk. He straightened up and waved the guard away.

"Y tu quien eres, preciosa?"

"Cristina. I can assure you, I'm much more interesting than estas dos y no te cuesto nada."

The blondes sitting at either side of Ricardo angrily looked at her with their mouths gaping, but Ricardo told his guards to have fun with the girls for the night.

"You've got some balls on you, muchacha. What if they threw their drinks at you?"

"Water doesn't bother a fish. No soy pendeja, me defiendo."

Ricardo pulled his head back and laughed. Cristina slowly drank her vodka martini and eventually pulled Ricardo from the VIP section and onto the dance floor. Despite his half-drunken state, he was a good dancer, Cristina thought. Cristina kept herself tight to him like a redback spider having caught its prey. They moved their hips and spun to the rhythm of bachata, merengue, and salsa. Julio caught Cristina from across the nightclub. He wanted to intervene, but the three men in black suits near Ricardo wouldn't allow that. He danced with random women, making sure to take a glance at Cristina every now and again. Seeing her like this, confident, unafraid, despite knowing who and what Ricardo was, both warmed and frightened him.

Near 3 a.m., Ricardo and Cristina left Paradise and started walking toward Ricardo's vehicle, where his chauffeur was waiting for them.

"Would you come home with me tonight, Cristina?"

"No se, I told my grandmother I'd come back home tonight. Ella esta enferma. I'm taking care of her, but she said to take the night and enjoy myself."

"Ah, pues, entiendo. Another time. I'll take you home."

As they pulled away, Cristina spotted Julio outside watching her. She lowered the window as they drove past him, smiled, and winked at him.

Julio took a long breath. *She's got this. I don't know how, but she's got this,* he thought.

They pulled up to a light blue house, accented with cream-colored patterns. Cristina went through her purse, feigned for the keys, and grabbed the fang, cloth first. Ricardo gently pulled on her arm and went in for a kiss. It was beer- and whiskey-laden, but she accepted and pulled him in by his jacket, slipping one hand inside its pocket.

"Hasta la proxima, Cristina," Ricardo said as his driver pulled away.

"Be seeing you, Ricardo."

Cristina walked inside to Dolores waiting in the darkness of the living room.

"Lo dejaste?"

"Si, it's in his jacket pocket."

"Bien hecho. La Baca necesita su sacrificio."

Cristina and Dolores sat and watched the midday news.

The reporter started, "Breaking News: Ricardo Aguilas, a prominent member of Santo Domingos' nightlife, and part owner of Paradise, and his driver have been found dead. The car was torn from the inside, its doors pulled off its hinges. The city coroner confirms large puncture wounds, teeth-like, and blunt trauma force to be the cause of death, though they are unclear if animals were involved. Police advise anyone in the area to be wary of—" Dolores clicked the TV off. The clothed fang hung where it always was.

Eyeliner ran down Cristina's face. "Gracias, Dolores. I couldn't do all this without you." Dolores put her hand on the small of Cristina's back and slowly rubbed. "Mija, I have so much more to teach you."

IT TAKES UN PUEBLO

Hector Duarte Jr.

El idiota del pueblo. That's what everyone calls me. I'm not stupid or anything. At least, I don't think I am. I see everything that's going on and why it happens. I don't talk much, and that's why I think people think I'm not all right. But, see, growing up in the village I did, you can't afford to run your mouth too much.

Nobody heard of my village until after 2015 when all the cartels started trying to take over the top half of Central America. Gracias al Señor is on the northern tip of Guatemala, right before you get to Mexico. Back in the day, when I was five or six, it was a place where road-tripping families stopped to stretch their legs and get some snacks for the road. I know because Dad used to run a fruit stand at "La Ultima Parada," a small cluster of huts that sold different specialties to passing tourists on the way to Azteclandia. These days, the marketplace no longer exists, and the nickname "La Ultima Parada" has a deadlier meaning attached to it. Cartels have made border crossing into Mexico a

147

notorious and dangerous business, which is why you might have heard of my village more recently.

Los Caza Cabezas are vying for power in the southern part of Mexico. They're small, not as small as when they first started back in 2015, but they're not as big as the Sinaloa Cartel. They're trying, though. The thing is, these boys ain't Mexican, but puro Guatemalteco. You think Mexican turf wars are violent? These Headhunters amp up their cruelty six, seven times over so Mexican drug lords take them extra seriously. Don't think "Headhunters" is just a cute nickname the media decided to give them, either. These nacos will cut the heads off their victims, stick dynamite in their mouths, and use the explosive heads to firebomb their next target. Remember my village now? Trust me, over the last three years, even if you don't remember hearing its ironic name, you've seen B-roll footage of its blood-soaked streets and mothers cursing the skies over the death of their too-young kid. Someone once told me I came out in the background, staring out into the street like a moron.

Here's the thing: I'm not a moron. I'm just extremely quiet, something my parents taught me when they were still alive. "Stay quiet, mijo, and watch what everyone else is doing. It makes for brilliant comedy." That was Dad, laughing at everyone while nobody knew he had the ability to smile. And Mom's mantra? "A buen entendedor, pocas palabras." If people are savvy enough, there ain't much explaining necessary. If it is necessary, it's probably not the kind of person you want around much anyway.

FOUR DEAD IN GUATEMALAN CHURCH FIREBOMBING

March 11, 2018

GRACIAS AL SEÑOR, Guatemala (GNA)—Locals have dubbed it "Los balazos santos" (holy bullets) after a group of three masked men entered the small church of Pedro de San Jose de Betancur and opened fire as the priest blessed the Eucharist.

The morning service had few participants, and most were able to scramble outside before the three men, all members of the notorious Caza Cabezas (Headhunters) Cartel, firebombed the altar using the decapitated heads of two local men who had previously gone missing. Father Reynaldo Souza was shot dead, while local residents Maria de Armas, Manuel Baldizon, and Efrain Rios Montt were all killed in the blast while attempting to escape.

"Father Reynaldo was breaking the body of Christ for all of us when someone at the back of the church shouted, 'Death to foreign invasion.' Next thing I know, the priest is dead over the altar and I'm running out. That's when I hear a huge explosion. By the time everyone could realize what had happened, they were gone," said Rigoberta Menchu, who signed the cross over and over as she spoke to reporters, repeating how lucky she was to be alive.

Gracias al Señor, and the northern portion of Guatemala in general, has seen a spike in violence over the last two years as local gangs respond to the threat of Mexican drug cartels expanding their territorial control into other Central American countries. It seems the Caza Cabezas, a strictly Guatemalan cartel, have changed their mission over the years, looking to carve out their own empire in Mexico, specifically in the city of San Cristobal de las Cazas on the country's southern border.

With all the power and allegiance shifts taking place in

this region on a daily basis, some are afraid to opine. Like one resident, who also witnessed Los Balazos Santos, promptly replied: "Yo no se nada." (I don't know anything).

This idiota's quote made the Guatemala News Agency's website. A few other media outlets found the quote clever and came around searching for me. It was mostly gringos looking for a cute story to dig out of all the shit we have going on out here. You know how hipsters do with their attention deficit; here a couple of days, asking about my routine, marveling at village life, going on and on about how they should take some of this home and teach Americans what it truly means to slow things down and live. Then, as soon as they come, they go. Back to their writing desks inside air-conditioned offices with unlimited coffee and Wi-Fi. I want to speed my life up, cabrones. Let's switch spots any day, even for just a week.

The church closed, and everyone wondered what would become of Betancur. Boarded up forever to become another stop on the walking tours? "This was the site of the Balazos Santos. Anyone remember hearing about it?"

Everyone at La Taverna Salamanca—our local, and only, watering hole—said what a shame about Father Reynaldo, how he would have kept it going, how someone should step in and do it for his honor to prove to los Caza Cabezas that this town would not be overrun with fear. Then they'd just take a shot of aguardiente and forget about the struggle.

I'm not religious. I go to church every morning because it's something to do in a place where there's not a lot to do. It fills a one-hour gap in an otherwise boring morning. We all know each other here and linger around after Mass talking to one another. It bonds us, but now with no one to head the church, and the local archdiocese scrambling to find a courageous priest to take over, we have nothing to do in the morning.

Had nothing to do in the morning, anyway. Two weeks after Gracias al Señor made the news and gringo crusaders came in trying to help, we had a new priest who stepped up and decided to be the church pastor. No one ever heard of the man before, and the bits and pieces people spoke about him seemed plucked out of mythology.

Hiram Astilla was from a mountainous region four hours north of Madrid that no one was looking for on a map. In Guatemala, we don't have the best view of Spaniards. In fact, we like to paint most of them as big-city faggots who spend too much time worrying about the whiteness of their teeth and the evenness of their hair. So when they heard the next Catholic import was Spanish, that was the image people painted in their heads. What they got instead was a hulking mass of a man over six feet tall with a huge beard covering the sides of his face and the point of his chin. I mean, this guy looked like the American Civil War President shot in a theater. He had met the regular pilgrims at church that morning. That afternoon, he walked in to La Taverna Salamanca in his priest's cassock and everyone had a hoot. They laughed even harder when he ordered a shot of American whiskey and chased it with a bottle of Miller.

Like always, I stayed quiet at the end of the bar furthest from the door, where the least amount of sunlight hits. I don't like people noticing me too much. It just makes it easier to observe everything that goes on. So, everyone is having a laugh at this man, when Osvaldo Cruz says so everyone can hear, "Drink up, Padre. With the fate that befalls every other priest who walks into this town, you do right numbing yourself."

The comment and the hearty laugh it got from everyone else did nothing to sway the Father. He flexed that shot back into his gullet and took a massive swig of the piss-yellow beer without souring his face in any way.

In seeing that, Osvaldo Cruz registered in the snap of a finger that here wasn't a man to mess with. This was the type of guy who made an example out of someone just to maintain stasis. Osvaldo Cruz had, in that moment, with those words, volunteered to be the model by which all other men in that town checked their behavior whenever they made even the smallest of comments toward Father Hiram Astilla.

The Father calmly turned to Osvaldo and extended a gentle, hulking hand. "Padre Hiram Astilla. Y tu?"

"Osvaldo Cruz," he said, gripping the big, holy, Paul Bunyan–hand tightly.

"Señor Cruz. It is a pleasure to meet someone who is so honest with someone they have never met before. That kind of honesty is simply rare these days, unfortunately. Wouldn't you say?"

Osvaldo held up his shot of aguardiente, said, "Here is to honesty," and took a swig.

"How long have you been here?" Astilla asked.

"My entire life. Fifty-three years."

"I mean, how long today have you been here in this bar?"

Osvaldo signaled the bartender with a smile. "What time do you guys open this dump?"

Astilla smiled as everyone laughed. "That's good but, see, unlike you, I am in here after a day's hard work, trying to do something with my life that helps others in return. Someone like you, who can only look forward each day to the opening of a bar, has made their life the size of a pin-hole because it is all you know. Me, and all the pilgrims who will help me rebuild the church, are actually doing something to help themselves and others."

The room was pin-drop quiet. I was one of those pilgrims helping out. Yulieta Arevalo was one of the regular churchgoers, and she sent the rest of us an email soon as she knew Astilla was coming to help rebuild. She said we should come help out to save face; no pressure, whatever kind of help anyone could contribute would be greatly appreciated. Upon meeting us, Father Astilla promised that the church would be open in one week, hell or high water.

I was surprised to see a priest in a bar, let alone holding his own against the village "badasses."

Osvaldo Cruz drank the rest of his aguardiente and seemed to wipe a tear from off his cheek. "Father, you are absolutely right. I want to apologize to you for criticizing."

Astilla smiled and slapped Osvaldo's back so hard, I heard the crystal-clear snap from the opposite end of the bar. "Don't apologize for the life you choose to live, man, but at least offer to buy me another round."

That sent up a huge huzzah, larger and more boisterous than any of Osvaldo's cheap quips had ever. It had that tone when very hypertension is suddenly undercut with general relief. When people are expecting a massive explosion to rip the room apart but at zero hour realize the fuse has been miraculously extinguished.

Osvaldo and a couple of his other drinking buddies were on hand the next day to help us remove bullets embedded in the church walls and pieces of splintered wood scattered through the whole church. Astilla mopped up the blood all by himself so the rest of us wouldn't have to see so much bloodshed. They say blood is very hard to clean up. If true, it must have taken him hours.

That night, we were invited to stay and hang out on the yard at the back of the church. Astilla gave us enough money to go to the market, buy chicken, veggies, and other greens. All of us ate and laughed like we hadn't never done at any gathering at La Taverna and especially never at church. Before that, there was never any playing around or laughing at church. That was the place God answered prayers, and if you wanted him to hear you, it better be damn quiet and respectful. At the end of the night, after much song and dance, Father Astilla told us to take the next day off and enjoy all the good work we had done and especially because no one had asked for our help. This priest didn't just preach, he did.

Halfway into my cup of coffee at La Taverna the next morning, Osvaldo walks in panting like he'd wrestled Kukulcan himself. "Father Astilla. Come quick."

Me and a couple of the guys shot up and stayed put until someone asked what no one wanted to. "They killed him?"

"No way. He didn't give them a chance to. You have to see this." The smile that crept over Osvaldo's face was none I'd ever seen before. And I'd seen that man in all kinds of emotional states, low to high. This, though, was the highest. A peak. We had to follow him.

Screams could be heard as we ran toward the corner of Iluminacion and Del Toro. There stood Astilla, bigger than ever. Is it possible to grow taller past your thirties?

His hands crossed across his double-barreled chest, a hammer in his left hand, and a massive smile over his face.

Nailed to the church door was a kid no more than twenty, arms stretched at either side like the Son of God himself. The kid wailed into the neighborhood with a gun laying at his feet, begging God and Astilla for mercy.

None of us who had gathered knew what to make of it.

"I hear a sound outside my living quarters this morning, like someone sneaking up on me." Astilla pointed to the kid who had stopped struggling to free himself. The blood trickled from the middle of his hands and collected into a puddle of blood surrounding both his feet. "Looks like the devil is trying to banish God right out of this town. But I work for God, and I refuse to let the devil have his way. Let's show them what happens in Gracias al Señor if they mess with our village. You've helped me rebuild the church, now I ask all of you to help me rebuild this city for good and all."

Usually when any priest spoke to us at Mass, we knew what was coming. All of us had gone to church so regularly through the years that we knew which passages fell on which days, and as much as the old priests tried to change up their homilies, they pretty much stayed the same. After a while of that, you stop listening. All of us were present and reverential in the Lord's presence, but hearing the same spiel time and again, it becomes easy to just stop listening, and that's what we did. But Father Astilla's message wasn't a typical homily plucked from the teachings of the good word. He didn't need the book tucked against his chest to move us into action; he just had to perform the action before anyone else did, and that was enough of a spark to get us going.

155

Osvaldo Cruz was the first to raise his fist in the air. "Let's take the town back and remind them who it really belongs to. They can scare one of us, but all of us will scare them."

"Are all of you of the same feeling?" Father Astilla asked.

The other barflies raised their hands in the air with a resounding, unified "Yes."

It sent a wave of energy through the rest of the group until everyone, including me, had their fists in the air.

Father Astilla turned to the sicario. "I am going to pull the nails from each one of your palms. You are going to go back to whatever hell you came from and tell them what happened here today. Make sure you let los Caza Cabezas know what kind of fight they are in for should they decide to come back."

"Please, Father. Have mercy and kill me now. You are only delaying the inevitable. They will make me suffer and then kill me. I beg you, show mercy and end my life now."

"The same way you were going to spare mine?" Father Astilla said before pulling the nail from the boy's right hand.

The kid's screams filled the church courtyard and the entire block until he passed out from pain. That was when Father Astilla removed the second nail. Osvaldo Cruz and three more of us dumped his unconscious body at the edge of the village where the cartel usually made their entrances and exits.

When a Jeep with four Headhunters came rolling up the street the next day, barreling in the direction of the church, we were ready for them. Father Astilla was on top of the church's bell tower with a sniper rifle aimed at the driver.

Osvaldo and his boys were hidden ground-level at different corners, ready to plug the whole crew. We had set up road spikes that me and the ladies would pull at either end when they got a certain distance from the church so they couldn't catch us off guard with any firebombs. The Jeep must have known, because it pulled a fast U-turn just before the spikes were set to go taut, and the passenger lobbed a decapitated head in the direction of the church. The Jeep's tires pealed off into the setting sun until it disappeared.

The head belonged to the kid from the day before. He'd been right. They wasted no time on him, and I could tell Father Astilla was angry about it. You know when someone is about to cry but doesn't want the tears to show? They swallow down hard against that lump in their throat that makes the tears want to come out even more. Instead of dynamite, they left a note in his mouth.

Mañana al mediodía, préndele a todos los santos una vela. Si Dios de veras existe, pronto lo conocerán.

Father Astilla read it aloud to all of us. When he was done, no one said a word. Crumbling the paper with a heavy, meaty fist, he tapped the spot over his chest three times and said, "Por mi culpa, por mi culpa, por mi gran culpa." Then he knelt right there by the boy's severed head and reverently prayed an Our Father and a Hail Mary. The women gathered into a circle around him and started a rosary that soon had the entire neighborhood praying. By the time we were done, the sun was barely lighting the sky. Father Astilla told us that whoever wanted to flee could; none of this was anybody's fight but his own. He started it and he would end it. All he wanted was to protect a small town from the outside world that was becoming more and more of an invader every day. "Leave town and come back when the news reports inform you of my death, but please know I do not do any of this to forsake you. I just cannot live in a world that pushes so many good people around. Save yourselves first and foremost."

Nobody moved, and Father Astilla stared at all of us like we were out of it until Tararo de la Paz, one of Osvaldo's cronies and the only one in town who could drink him under the table, stepped forward and said to all those gathered, "The note says *if* God exists. God does exist. A year ago, none of us would have been out here fighting for the same reason. We've been living together for our entire lives, and this is the first time we all gather together to fight the same fight when normally we're just bickering with one another. If all of us here together is not a sign that God exists, then I don't know what is." He pointed to Father Astilla. "This man is responsible for this, and I'm not about to just leave him on his own to fight for a town that tried laughing him away when he first came through."

Tararo walked over, stood next to the Father, and wrapped his arm tightly around his shoulder.

It just takes one ripple, you know, for people to follow examples. And that's what we all did. All of us. Just like Tararo, we stood by the Father. I was one of the first ones so people don't think I'm a follower. I know a lot of them expected me to join last, and that's why I didn't. I'm not as simple as they are convinced I am.

Just like the night we all celebrated together, we gathered in the yard between the church and Astilla's living quarters. We ate and drank like that last time, but instead of partying, we talked strategy. Huddled in clusters, we talked about what each of us would do tomorrow when the cartel came to fight. There were a lot of us, each one good at something the others didn't know about. We could attack them from the ground or from up high. Combined as one, we were unstoppable. We had planned and were prepared, come what may. We'd taken a village no one knew about and turned it into a group of fighters that people would speak about; that was victory enough. Even if we lost, we'd win.

With nothing to lose, we conversed in that yard like the best thinkers and planners you read about in history books, but it was live; we were making something happen. Around here, that kind of thinking is rare. Tell me the last time a village had enough integrity to go against an entire cartel? Without some fucking chibato—getting ten pesos a week from one of the cartel's bottom men—ratting out an uprising. We may have been "a little shit-splat town" who was up in each other's business, and we bickered because of it, but we took that same energy and turned it into our own militia that knew the lay of the land and could fight any cartel the fuck out. To them, we were just a speck on the map, but we knew they needed us to expand. Without us, their story ends where ours began. Plain and simple.

If we lost, the next village would be even bigger, with people who maybe hated each other a little more but now knew what the cartel brought so they planned a little better and fought a little harder. Then, guess what? The cartel ain't so fucking big and bad anymore. Then, two villages join forces and those become three and, guess what? Now, the small militia turns into an army, motherfucker. An army that crushes the fuck out of every corrupt-ass politician taking kickbacks. An army that takes back all of Central and South America to what it once was and what it could be. A place where North Americans would illegally cross their own borders to come here, and not vice versa, because we have the best jobs, natural resources, and opportunity to live the American Dream that North Americans think only exists and is possible on their side of the line. The kind of place where you would want to retire because, guess what? Here, the ocean still has that certain shade of blue you remember the water had back when you were how old? Where you can park anywhere on the street to get to a beautiful slice of ocean without having to pay ten dollars an hour then circumnavigate five skyscrapers and a hipster obstacle course before your toes touch sand. We were going to make Centroamérica great again or die trying.

Later in the night, when things started to cool down and the conversation slowed like it does when everyone knows it's getting late and closer to the time to call it a night, maybe the last night for all of us, Father Astilla and me made eye contact. We smiled, nodded at one another, and he winked at me like we were the only two people in the world, sharing an inside joke no one else was privy to.

The next morning, as the Caza Cabezas' rusted-out Jeeps made their way into Gracias al Señor and up Iluminacion to the church, we readied ourselves to show them just what they were walking into.

The first Jeep took the improvised explosive Tararo set up in the middle of the road. That was the plan. We didn't have enough munitions to take out the entire cavalry, but we blindsided them by blowing the shit out of that first one. In a flash of twisted green metal, the car split in half, sending the limbs and bloody parts of the three soldiers in it flying every which way. The second car stopped just long enough—the guys inside no doubt wondering what the hell was happening—for Osvaldo Cruz, perched atop the church bell tower, to slice a bullet into the driver's and passenger's throats. The two guys in the back got out and ran in the opposite direction, because cartel money stacks only so high with a sniper rifle trained on the back of your head. Cruz was able to pop the back of one of their heads off, but next thing we knew, a guy in the third Jeep got out with a grenade launcher and made rubble out of the sniper tower. It would take hours to find Cruz's body underneath all the rubble.

Father Astilla let out a guttural scream like he had just witnessed the death of Jesus Christ himself and made Swiss cheese out of the Jeep, but by that time the two guys had hidden behind the walls of the general store just up the block as three more Jeeps pulled in from the distance, kicking up dirt and dust we had littered with blood, sweat, and…shit…You know the rest. We were holding it together, but it's scary in that moment, realizing the last vision of your fading life might be staring up into the hot sun while your guts and intestines bleed out from the hit they took off a cartel artillery shell. ISIS and Charlottesville, my ass. We've been getting rolled over by domestic terrorism since I can remember.

Then, blam! A piercing hot bullet ripped into my left shoulder. I don't know if that's the way bullets go, or if there was so much intensity happening that at first I didn't feel anything, until Father Astilla lifted me by the left arm-pit with Tararo carrying my legs. They carried me into the church with Yulieta Arevalo and the rest of her crew providing cover fire.

The Caza Cabezas had us cornered inside Betancur with two choices: get firebombed or go down in a blaze of glory. We all looked at each other with a smile and a nod, just like the night before, knowing this would be our last stand. The church and each of our faces would be the last snippets of consciousness we'd take up to Heaven with us. The best we could do was hope and pray our original mission did exactly what it needed to do: give others the example to fight their own cartels, only with enough preparation to push the narcos away and win back their village.

"Put me down and help me up," I said.

"What are you doing? Stay down," Father Astilla begged.

"You need all the help you can get. I have two choices right now. Die in here laying on the steps to the altar or die out there fighting on the steps to the church. What do they both have in common? I die."

Father Astilla looked at all of us. We'd lost just one man, but the numbers out there would no doubt crush the numbers in here. "I want you all to know that I just—"

"Shhh," Yulieta commanded. "I may be seeing you guys at the Pearly Gates in no time, but while we're still here, let's give these assholes hell."

Several explosions rocked the church floor and sent us ducking for cover. We ran behind one of the only stained-glass windows still intact. There were four cartel Jeeps at the center of the street, but they had been surrounded by trucks I recognized from all over Gracias al Señor.

The town recluses had surrounded our invaders. Jose Maria Holnes was out there. His wife had died over twenty years earlier from brain cancer, and he hadn't come out of his house since, except to buy groceries. The town talked about one famous episode where Osvaldo Cruz tried to stop him in one of the aisles just to make sure he was okay, and Holnes clipped him with a strong punch to the left side of his face that left a shiner visible from the other end of town. Whenever we were drunk enough at Salamanca, we gave Cruz so much shit over that. Now, Holnes was at the front lines with Miguel Baratonez; Xavier Cuenca; his girlfriend, Ynez de la Flor; and Michael Schumer, who had retired here from Oxnard, California eleven years back when he became bored with the North American grind. The entire village came out, and it outnumbered the cartel.

Those guys didn't know what to do with themselves, except look around confused like a bunch of caged circus animals. In less than ten seconds, we mowed down the entire convoy with bullets, bombs, and everything we had until the spot where they'd stood was a smoking heap of metal, gristle, bone, and muscle. We smoked them right out of their fucking hole. The smell coming out of there was like pig fat coming out of the most intense, festive barbeque you can imagine.

There was one more Jeep coming up out of the distance. Just one. We stood in line-formation blocking the street. Without slowing down, the Jeep busted a U and headed back out into the desert until it faded into the sun.

We lifted Father Astilla on our shoulders and celebrated like it was the second coming of Christ. It was only about a minute before he tapped me on the shoulder and said to put him down. He didn't believe in celebrating it as his idea when all of us were just as responsible for the good work done that day. He called it God's work.

When we put him down, he thanked all of us and said it

wasn't over. "They will come back. Who knows when? But they'll be back, and they will come back with five times the force they showed now. We need to be ready and stick together. Don't get lazy."

He said that almost a week ago, and so far we haven't seen any action. We made the news and told the international media we had no idea what might happen tomorrow. People have started coming in from the nearby parts of Guatemala, Honduras, Mexico, and even the U.S. People who just want to fight any kind of fight and have never had the opportunity. Some of them have even talked about staying full-time to protect Gracias al Señor.

Some of the old-school villagers complain, but the way I see it, this is the most attention our village has ever gotten. We've done the impossible. Went from little-known, "shit-splat town" to guerilla fighters who gather people from all over the world who one month ago wouldn't have been able to locate the Guatemala-Mexico border on a map. We've made a name for ourselves, not by housing and selling out to the cartel but by fighting the enemy, pushing it away, and letting it know that if it came back, this little Guatemalan village would give it hell. And we had a fucking army of citizens backing us up. Whatever invasor came back, it would have to shoot down hard-working, old-school villagers—the very people cartels need to expand territory—in front of a live, international audience. Did it have the balls to do it? Yeah.

We're here, though, waiting to hit back if it does, to show the entire world just what Gracias al Señor is made of. That's one thing I know with certainty.

RED ZONE
ALEX SEGURA

"We are completely fucked."

Raul Alvarez heard the words over the crowd—the boos growing in intensity as he walked from the huddle to the line of scrimmage. He tugged on his helmet—a tic he'd had since he first played tackle football as a kid. For fun. It was fun then.

The words had come from his own side—the center, Tommy Detmer, a big, bruising lineman who never gave up a sack. He was a rock. Loyal. Violent in the scrum. He also hated Raul's guts.

The "why" of that equation baffled Raul. At least in terms of logic. There was none. Raul was quiet, kept to himself, did what was asked of him at practice, and didn't socialize much. The Southern Florida University Red Wolves were 5-2 and needed to run the table if they had any chance of winning their division—the Southern USA Athletic Conference, part of the NCAA's Division III, which was just a fancy way of saying "schools that played football but didn't give scholarships."

Raul walked up to the line of scrimmage and took his

spot behind Detmer. He scanned the defense's formation. They were facing the Brevard College Tornados, a team known for a swarming defense and a run, run, then run some more offensive philosophy. There were ten minutes left in the fourth quarter, and the Red Wolves were down by fourteen. Not an ideal situation for a rarely used back-up quarterback to step onto the field. Even less ideal when you were hated by most of your teammates.

The safeties were in—meaning they were going to blitz or at least make Raul think they were. He looked to his left—Terrell Malcolm, the team's speedy top receiving option, was out wide. Raul looked right. Charlie Evans, a solid possession receiver who might have trouble outrunning a sloth, was in the slot. Both were solid route-runners. Both knew what was at stake. Raul just hoped he had the skills to get one of them the ball.

"Set..." Raul said, his voice loud and clear. It was now or never.

"You ever seen a spic quarterback?"

The words slid into Raul's ears and pierced his brain. He turned and noticed the source. Danny Mathers, the Red Wolves senior starter. Everything about him said QB—tall, well-built, thick-jawed, and a trademark goofball smile. But from this angle, the toothy grin had an air of something more sinister. Raul watched as Danny looked Raul's way, saw the flicker of realization in his face as he realized Raul had heard, then gave an almost imperceptible shrug.

Detmer, the intended recipient of Danny's snide comment, chuckled as the two passed Raul, who was heading onto the field for his turn running the offense in practice.

As the backup QB, Raul got little time behind center—just enough so he wouldn't be lost if he ever had to enter a game (God forbid), but not too much. No one wanted a quarterback controversy. Plus, there wasn't one. Danny had flunked out of a Division I school and was slumming with the Red Wolves until he got his academics in order enough to transfer. But as long as he was around, he was the only quarterback that mattered.

Raul opened his mouth, as if ready to respond, but thought better of it. Then he felt the hand on his shoulder—rough, pulling him back, and forcing him to turn.

"You got something to say, rafter?" Detmer's voice lowered an octave. He squared up, nostrils flaring, Danny standing behind him—that stupid, sly smirk almost glowing on Danny's face.

Raul could feel Detmer's hot breath on his face now. Could feel his own face reddening with shame.

"No," Raul said. "I don't."

"S'what I thought," Detmer said, backing up, then turning around and almost skipping toward Danny as they made a beeline for the bench. The starters rarely watched the second-stringers practice. What for?

Raul took the snap and did a quick three-step drop. He saw Evans on the periphery of his vision making a sharp cut across the field just as the safeties committed to the blitz, overpowering the Red Wolves' schizophrenic offensive line. Raul released the pass a second before a mammoth defensive lineman brought him down. He felt his helmet slam onto the faded, brown-green grass. Saw the Red Wolves sideline vibrate as he bounced back up from the impact. He let himself lay on his back for a second, then heard the roar of the crowd. Nothing huge, but enough. He knew the pass was complete.

First down.

"Raul?"

His abuelo's voice shook him back to the present. Back to his front porch in Miami. Back to summer. Back to thinking about his life. His bruised body. The taunts. The environment. The world he'd left—familiar, comfortable, more like him—and the world he'd chosen—distant, achingly white, and foreign to him.

"What are you doing out here, mijo? It's late. Did something happen?"

"No, nada, nothing, abu," Raul said, standing up and walking up the porch steps briskly. He gave his elderly grandfather a warm hug and kiss on the cheek. "Todo bien."

"I wasn't expecting you tonight," abuelo Alfredo said, his smile wide but a bit shaky. He knew something was up, and he was fishing for it. Hard. "Are you back...for good?"

Raul paused for a moment before responding. *Was he?*

"No," he said, with more firmness than he felt. "I'm going back in a week. Summer practices are starting, and I want to get my reps in."

His abuelo nodded slowly. Understanding *why* Raul was doing it even if he didn't accept it.

Why be with people who hate you, Raul? Why play this game that has nothing to do with you or who we are? I didn't escape Cuba for that. I left for you—your mother, your entire family—to be happy. Fulfilled in this great country. Not despised.

The argument had been brief, heated, and jarring. Raul thought back to it often, especially in his lowest moments, when he doubted every aspect of his decision. Why had he chosen to go to school in the middle of Florida, far from his mama's arroz con pollo, far from his friends, far from his family—just to ride the bench on a football team that was a blip on the radar, with no chance at anything beyond a few stories after graduation?

His abuelo, five or six inches shorter than Raul, wrapped an arm around his grandson's shoulder and ushered him into the house.

"Tengo un poco de picadillo," he said, referencing Raul's favorite dish—ground beef, heavily seasoned and mixed with a variety of delectable ingredients. "Tienes hambre?"

"Abuelo, siempre tengo hambre."

21-28. Down by seven. Two-minute warning. Red Wolves' ball on their own thirty.

Raul stood up from the bench. He looked down the sideline. The medics had come back from the locker room. The word was out. Danny Mathers was done. Knee blown out. Done for the game's remaining two minutes. For the season. Maybe forever.

Art Schenker, the Red Wolves head coach—a stocky, well-built man with a bullfrog's demeanor—moved toward Raul, eyes on his iPad display. When he got within a foot of Raul, he looked up.

"You got this, Alvarez?"

Raul nodded at the coach before looking onto the field. He watched as the eleven men who made up the Red Wolves' offensive team sauntered toward what could be their last meaningful drive of the season. Or the beginning of the rest of one.

"Yeah, Coach, yeah," Raul said, sliding his helmet on. "I got this."

"Jeez, you're a lifesaver, Raul," Jennifer Reed said, her smile soft and warm. Her amber hair framing her wide eyes and sharp features. "I don't know how I'd pass this class without you. I feel like such a dumbass."

"Don't say that. Of course you'd pass," Raul said, a forced chuckle inserted for good measure. "I'm just helping you get there faster."

The remnants of their Chemistry and Society class had all but filtered out of the lab, leaving them alone at their shared desk.

She leaned forward, her face next to his. He could smell her tangy perfume, feel her cheek brush on his. She kissed his cheek—not a casual hi/bye peck, but a kiss, her lips lingering on his face in a way that, to Raul, felt like so much more than it actually was. But he could dream. Hell, he would dream about this for a long time.

She pulled back, smiling that soft smile.

"See you at the party?"

Raul started to reply but stammered out of the gate.

"Please tell me you're coming," Jennifer said, mock surprise on her face, her hand resting on his leg. A touch that ran hot through Raul's body—like sweet torture. "It's gonna be great. Trust me. It won't be boring. Nothing I do is boring."

She got up and slung her small black backpack over her shoulders. She gave him a friendly shove.

"See you there, buddy."

He watched her walk out of the classroom and let out a long sigh.

"What the fuck are you doing?" he said to himself as he started to slide his books into his bag. He heard the door swing open. She was back, he figured. Forgot something, like she always did.

"Left your pen?" Raul said, turning around. That's when he noticed it wasn't Jennifer. It was Detmer. And Danny Mathers. As in her boyfriend, Danny Mathers.

Shit.

"You got some balls on you, Speedy Gonzales," Detmer said, grabbing Raul's bag and tossing it across the room. "Some serious—what do you taco-eaters call it? Cojones? Yeah, that's it." He pronounced the 'j' as in jack—accentuated it on purpose.

"Guys, what—what is this?" Raul said, annoyed now, his patient veneer cracking.

The emotions he'd been feeling—the desire and attraction, the lust and delirium, had morphed into anger and disappointment. *Who the fuck did these guys think they were?*

Mathers said nothing. No "that's my fucking girlfriend, bro" or "keep your hands off my woman"—nothing like that. Raul would've almost appreciated something, anything that felt human. Instead, the quarterback leaned against the teacher's empty podium and watched.

Detmer came at him fast and hard, like the deceptively fast lineman he was—his tree-trunk arms grabbing him by the shirt and slamming him back onto the table behind him.

Raul didn't fight back. Didn't swing. Didn't kick. Didn't use the ruler within arm's reach to gouge Detmer's eyes out. He took it. He realized this after the fact, as he sat in the nurse's station, declining to answer her repeated questions about "what happened?" and "you should really go to the hospital..." Why? Why hadn't he fought this monster, this lumbering oaf? Raul didn't know. He just knew—felt deep inside himself—that sliding down to their level...fighting like animals without any other recourse, responding to their hate with his own...was not the path he'd been raised to take.

Raul tried to hold him off but was instantly overpowered and overwhelmed—the first fist cut through his meager defenses, crashing into his face like a giant hammer. Then another punch to the stomach. Raul felt his body crumple to the ground as another fist connected with his skull. Then things went gray and brown. When he could open his eyes, he was on the floor. He saw blood on his shirt and felt an aching pain spread over his face and midsection.

"Learn your fucking lesson, Pancho," Mathers said, his black boots sliding briefly on the streak of dark red blood on the linoleum floor. Raul's blood.

My blood.

27-28. No time left on the clock.

Coach Schenker decided to go for two points rather than an extra point for the tie. A tie wouldn't get them in the playoffs, but it wouldn't be an "L." Schenker didn't play for ties, though. Raul knew that.

"We win or we die," Schenker said as he slapped Raul's helmet hard with his palm, his face close—so close Raul could smell the cheap whiskey and cheaper aftershave.

Raul nodded and took the field. The team was waiting,

in an I-formation, the halfback and fullback lined up behind him. There was no need for a huddle here. They knew the play. Had known it since the season started. The only difference was who was captaining the ship.

Raul stepped toward Detmer and looked down at the center, a giant, glowering mass of anger and muscle gripping the football that needed to cross a certain line or send the entire season into oblivion. Raul saw Detmer's head turn slightly, and their eyes met.

"Danny's gone, man," Detmer said, loud enough for the entire team to hear. "This is all you, Alvarez. We're riding on your back tonight. Can you carry us?"

Detmer's message was a potent mix of bravado, apology, and confidence. Raul nodded and settled in behind Detmer. He looked around at the players. Some looked back. The opposing defense seemed to snarl at them. They knew it was all on the line here, their season and the Red Wolves'. For a college football division that many seemed to write off, for a game that most college football fans in the nation didn't think mattered—it sure as hell felt important.

"You're on my back right now," Raul said, loudly, his voice taking on a decibel he'd never felt before. "We got this, all right?"

He saw the nods. Detmer's sly smile as he turned to face the opposing defensive tackle and said something gruesome about his mother. Saw Terrell Malcolm rub his hands together in anticipation. This was it, Raul thought. And nothing else mattered. Not the flying punches or the garbage talk from Detmer or Mather's misplaced jealousy. Not coach's drinking problem or the call Raul had gotten before the game—the one that let him know his abuelo had died quietly in his sleep in a hospital in Miami. No. What mattered was this play, this moment.

He took the snap and dropped back, rolling right. Evans was covered, his lead feet keeping him close to the line of scrimmage. Their star running back, Deshon Avery, had gone off route and paid the price—a speedy linebacker on him like a basement cobweb. But there was Malcolm, a half-step ahead of the Tornados' drowsy corner, dragging. The game had been long; everyone was tired. He was hoping Raul wouldn't see him asleep at the wheel.

Raul Alvarez let rip with a tight spiral and watched it head toward Malcolm's long, outstretched hands, his feet resting on his toes, on the fringe of the end zone's far right side.

BORICUA OBITUARY
CINA PELAYO

"All died yesterday today
and will die again tomorrow. "
—Puerto Rican Obituary, Pedro Pietri

If you went out at night, you saw ghosts. That's what my father told me. He grew up in Puerto Rico in the 1940s in Adjuntas, a small mountain town that was once known for producing coffee and sugar cane. Today, everyone wants to get off of that mountain. My father left when he was sixteen years old with twenty dollars in his pockets and took a plane alone for the first time to New Jersey. He went with the Puerto Rican Farm Labor Program. It worked in tandem with the Bracero program you may have heard of before. Bracero worked with Mexican labor. Same concept. Cheap labor, brown people. My father worked on that farm in New Jersey one day before leaving. The work was too hard, and he wanted to be in a city, not on a farm. He met up with a cousin in Brooklyn and started washing dishes at restaurants he could never afford to eat at himself. It was his Black co-workers who taught him

English, and to the African American community I'll eternally be grateful for the kindness they showed to my dad, that mountain boy from a town of ghosts who was all alone on the mainland but for some few distant cousins.

Puerto Rican's don't die. We leave this here place, this out there place, this in-between place, and we finally go back to our island home as coquis. And every time you hear one of those tiny tree frogs' brilliant whistle cutting through the dark jungle at night, know that's the sound of your ancestors welcoming you back home. I think it's something we all who have been born on the island psych ourselves into believing, that we'll go back to our Borinquen and that we'll die on our island. Isn't that what the lyrics of En Mi Viejo San Juan are all about?

Pero un dia volvere
A buscar mi querer
A sonar otra vez
En mi viejo San Juan

That's not what happened though. My dad left Puerto Rico for the mainland. He married. Had three children and had a life here. My dad was then killed in Chicago, murdered—in the winter. He was laid to rest in Rosehill Cemetery, in the city, and when the ground was no longer frozen, he was buried. There is a simple headstone with his name.

And now that I'm ready and my brothers are ready, it's time to face one another after all of these years and admit which one of us killed him.

Cancer is a mother fucker. You're feeling great one day. You go in for some prescribed yearly checkup. They find something. They send you for another checkup with some other doctor, and then goddamn it, it's cancer. My dad was seventy-eight when he was diagnosed with prostate cancer. The night my brothers found out, my brother Richard went downstairs late at night and watched him sleep. Richard was forty years old at the time and of course living upstairs from my parents. Roberto Jr. was fifty years old, and he naturally lived in the basement.

I text Coco, which is what we called Richard, because every Puerto Rican has a Puerto Rican nickname. So, I text Coco that night of my dad's diagnosis and I told him: *Bro stop crying in front of dad.*

He responded that he wasn't crying.

I was like: *Motherfucker, you're watching him sleep. Stop it. You're freaking him out.*

That's the last I heard of Coco watching my dad sleep, but I'm sure he continued to do it up until the day Dad died. Coco was like that. He didn't understand, or maybe he didn't believe my parents' mortality. I had been telling him for years that they were getting older. They weren't young anymore, but it was like he and Tito, Roberto Jr.'s Puerto Rican nickname, were oblivious and so continued taking advantage of my parents. The boys didn't pay rent, ever. The boys didn't clean their own apartments, ever. The boys were tended to by my parents like they were children. Those grown-ass, lazy men.

Right after dad was diagnosed, I called my mom one day, and she was crying. I told her she better not be crying in front of Dad. She said he had just left the house to go get his numbers, his weekly lotto ticket, and that it was the first time she could cry. She told me she was scared. She told me she didn't know what to do. I told her there was nothing she could do. All we could do was make sure he was comfortable. She told me she was happy that I was married with kids and that Coco was about to marry some Dominican girl and Tito, even though he was separated from his wife for over ten years and still refused to pay for a divorce because he was too cheap, had his adult kids Yaya and Frankie.

The doctors told my dad that he needed chemotherapy every day for seven weeks. You know what my dad said when he heard that? *I ain't going.* And you know what? I didn't blame him. It was his life. It was his choice to live out his life the way he wanted to live it. My dad, who had already had back-to-back strokes ten years prior, and I swear he didn't die then because I pulled every brujeria trick I had, knew that he was lucky to have gotten those extra ten.

My mom's a pretty cold lady normally. So when I heard her cry, I knew she was really worried. My mother is Catholic as hell. Like, growing up, when I would go to the kitchen late at night for food, she'd be sitting there at the kitchen table reading the Bible. She also had this three-foot statue of Jesus she found in the old brownstone her and my dad used to live in before the old neighborhood got gentrified. She kept that shit right in the sala, by the TV. She would light a candle in front of that statue regularly and kneel and pray right there asking Jesus Christo for I don't know what, because everything that came out of her mouth in prayer was a soft whisper. You know what it's like walking out of your bedroom as a kid, into a dark sala, and your mother is there kneeling in front of a three-foot Jesus with a novena candle flame flickering shadows across her face? No. It freaked me the fuck out.

My dad wasn't Catholic. My dad wasn't anything. When I asked him if his parents believed in God, he said those people didn't believe in anything. I have clear memories of going to church every Sunday as a kid because my mom forced all of us, except Tito. There was my mom standing up, sitting down, and genuflecting whenever the priest said to with my dad just sitting there the entire time in his black suit. That's one thing about Dad, he always dressed sharp. My dad looked like Dean Martin with Sammy Davis Jr.'s swag. My dad loved the Rat Pack.

I don't know how my dad wound up in Chicago. Hell, I don't think most people know how the hell they wind up in Chicago. They just get stuck here, and the cold clamps down on you and you're fucked. You hate it here but can't leave. I knew my parents met here. My mom from some uppity Puerto Rican town hated my dad's mountain, jibaro family. So we never saw my dad's family. My dad was the only member of his family here. He had no one here but us, and I'm sure my mom liked it that way.

My dad told me about going to work downtown at the factories, and yes, before the multimillion-dollar condos, there were the factories. My dad told me about riding the elevated train on the way to his job, in his nice suit—because even though he worked in a factory, my man wore a suit. He'd sometimes see a co-worker on the El, but for fear of people hearing them speak Spanish, or even hearing their accents, they didn't acknowledge each other. But here's the thing: my dad was Chicago. My dad was State Street that Great Street. My dad was Madison Avenue and Wrigley Field and Comiskey Park. My dad was Chicago, Chicago that toddlin' town.

I knew our house was haunted growing up when I

started hearing people running back and forth upstairs when there was no one else up there. You'd hear doors slamming too. When I asked my dad about the noise up there, when no one else was up there, he told me never to mention it again. He said you don't talk about those things. It gives it power to talk about those things.

Before I started kindergarten, sometimes my dad would take me out with him. We'd ride the El, and we'd go to the bars in Humboldt Park and meet up with his fellas, and they'd drink at the bar, and his dudes would give me quarters and I'd play Pac-Man arcade. Sometimes, though, my father wouldn't take me with him. He'd leave me at home alone when he stepped out to run quick errands. When my grandfather and aunt and cousins weren't upstairs, I'd hear the running back and forth and the doors slamming. One day, I heard the door of our apartment open, all the while the running back and forth was going on. It was this crazy rumbling, and I remember being huddled behind my parents' bed, and I swear on my life something grabbed my shoulder and I've never been so afraid. When my dad came back home, he was my goddamn hero. I threw my arms around him and screamed and cried so hard. He never left me alone again.

When my dad was dying, I promised never to leave him alone either. He told me stories, so many stories those last few months, that I wondered why my dad didn't mean more to other people. My dad told me about the Division Street race riots and how he was attacked by an officer's German shepherd and sprayed with a firehose. He told me how one time he stopped in the Italian neighborhood at a diner to get a cup of coffee. He ordered his coffee by simply saying "coffee" but that was enough to give his otherness away. The waitress told him to finish up his coffee and get out unless he wanted trouble.

First day of college, my dad drove me. My wedding day, Dad walked me down the aisle, drunk as hell, but he managed, even though he couldn't finish the daddy-daughter dance since he had so much Bacardi in him. My father was my everything, and here this thing came to destroy him. A man who had survived every setup against him because of what he was, what he sounded like, and what he looked like was literally being eaten away by his own body.

When Hurricane Maria hit, that broke him. His mother was still alive, in her late 90s, and so was his sister and a couple of nephews. There's nothing like the desperation of knowing your home is being destroyed and those you love cannot be reached by any form of communication. It was almost like the hurricane had taken a piece of him when he saw the flyover images of how devastated the land was. It was about a year after my dad was diagnosed, and a short time after when he told me about the banana ghost and the lanterns.

One night, when he was a little boy, he left his small wooden house in the mountains at night and walked toward the latrine. When he was done, he walked past a banana tree and saw that a banana was ripe. He reached for it, but it escaped his grasp. He thought it was the dark or his sleepiness and he reached again, but it didn't meet his hand. The leaves of the tree were shaking. The bananas were shaking. Tempting him closer. He took another step forward, and that's when he heard his mother call him from behind, grabbing him by his shoulders and asking him what he was doing. He looked back at the tree and then he looked down. His feet were at the edge of the mountain and one more step would have killed him.

My dad liked to dance. He liked to party. He drank until the day he died. He started young, and he said when he would go out at night in his teens, he would take a lantern with him. All of the kids took lanterns with them. It was the 1940s, in rural Puerto Rico. After their parties, the kids would light their lanterns and walk back up the mountain toward their home. My dad said that on some nights, when you walked up the mountain alone with your lantern, you would see the ghosts of people walking up the mountain, their lanterns lit in the darkness. They too were walking home.

I wondered why he told me those stories. He told me not to talk about those things when I was younger because talking about those things would give it power. Maybe he just knew his time was ending. Maybe he knew it was time to give those things, those ghostly, unknown things power.

So, coming here now, after so many years after my father's death, I thought it was fitting to bring a lantern with me. A flight to San Juan and a two-hour drive up the winding mountain road to see my brothers who had too traveled here from stateside. I had not seen them in twenty years. We had agreed to meet here, as soon as one of us learned they were dying. We would all come up here, to this mountain, to my grandfather's old wooden house—likely consumed by the mountain—and admit which one of us had pulled our father's oxygen mask off of his face. Admit which one of us had turned off all of his machines and admit which one of us had killed him. Yes, he was going to die, but which one of us had taken whatever few minutes or hours or days from him.

In retrospect, it was a stupid agreement. What if one of

us got killed in a car accident or died of a heart attack? Then we'd never know which one of us killed him.

It didn't matter now because here we all here. We had kept our promise. Birthdays and holidays had passed, and we didn't even reach out to each other. When I learned I was dying, I reached out to them both and told them it was time for us to meet. I saw them now in the distance. Two rental cars parked alongside this green mountain road. A crumbling, wooden structure tucked behind great banana trees and coffee beans was once the house our father had grown up in. My grandfather's house. The same house where he sat on the porch and waved to travelers all day. The same porch where he looked at me when I was a teenager girl and laughed and said "Te estoy velando." I wondered now if my grandfather and father were watching me. Mountain ghosts.

Twenty years is a long time. My brothers and I hated each other, but we were born of this mountain. We were born from a man and a woman who didn't even know the names of their great-grandparents. We were born of a man and a woman who were raised in houses with dirt floors. We were born of a man and a woman who didn't complete school beyond the sixth grade, whose parents never learned to read or write. But my brothers and I had done well for ourselves. One brother I had heard was very wealthy, beyond a millionaire, and the other had just retired from his job at the hospital as a nurse. My father must have been proud of what that twenty dollars in his pocket had got him.

When I opened the car door and stepped out, I couldn't do anything but collapse and cry because they both looked so much like him, so much like my favorite person. They both looked like that man who would dance salsa with me in the kitchen when I was five years old, that old Zenith radio blaring. They both looked like the man who would roast a pernil on Christmas day. They both looked like the man who worked in factories until he could no longer work because his crushing anxiety kept him at home. They both looked like the man who enjoyed a cup of coffee in the morning with a slice of French bread alongside his newspaper. They both looked like the man who took me to the Puerto Rican Day Parade in Chicago for the first time and sat me on his shoulders so I could watch the floats driving by. They both looked like the man who had taken me to Puerto Rico for the first time and who looked over at me as the plane landed and applauded and smiled because he was back home.

"I did it," I said through tears. "I killed him because I could not see him in pain anymore. I never wanted him to feel any pain, and I took that away and I'm not sorry. I'm not sorry I took away his pain."

And through the tears, I couldn't see anything. I could only feel my brothers hugging me and crying with me, and in the distance, I could hear the song of the coquis.

ACKNOWLEDGMENTS

To the writers who chose to gift this project with their wonderful stories—I thank you. I only wish I could have done a little more, but I don't think we're done here.

ABOUT THE CONTRIBUTORS

CHANTEL ACEVEDO'S novels include *Love and Ghost Letters* (St. Martin's Press), which won the Latino International Book Award and was a finalist for the Connecticut Book of the Year, *Song of the Red Cloak*, a historical novel for young adults, *A Falling Star* (Carolina Wren Press), winner of the Doris Bakwin Award, and National Bronze Medal IPPY Award, and *The Distant Marvels*, (Europa Editions), one of Booklist's Top Ten Historical Novels of 2015. *The Living Infinite*, a novel about the Infanta Eulalia, was published by Europa Editions in 2017. Acevedo is currently an Associate Professor of English in the MFA Program of the University of Miami.

HECTOR ACOSTA was born in Mexico City and moved to the United States. He spent time in El Paso and Dallas before moving with his understanding wife and dog to New York. His time living on the border left an impression on him, and much of his writing revolves around that area and its people. In his free time he enjoys watching wrestling and satisfying a crippling Lego addiction.

A Mexican-American author from deep South Texas, **DAVID BOWLES** is an assistant professor at the University of Texas Rio Grande Valley. Recipient of awards from the American Library Association, Texas Institute of Letters and Texas Associated Press, he has written a dozen or so books, including *Flower, Song, Dance: Aztec and Mayan Poetry*, the critically acclaimed *Feathered Serpent, Dark Heart of Sky: Mexican Myths*, and *They Call Me Güero:*

A Border Kid's Poems. In 2019, Penguin will publish *The Chupacabras of the Rio Grande* co-written with Adam Gidwitz, and Tu Books will release his steampunk graphic novel *Clockwork Curandera*. His work has also appeared in multiple venues such as *Journal of Children's Literature*, *Rattle*, *Strange Horizons*, *Apex Magazine*, *Nightmare*, *Asymptote*, *Translation Review*, *Metamorphoses*, *Huizache*, *Eye to the Telescope*, and *Southwestern American Literature*. In April 2017, David was inducted into the Texas Institute of Letters for his literary work.

ANGEL LUIS COLÓN is the Derringer and Anthony Award shortlisted author of *Hell Chose Me*, the Blacky Jaguar novella series, the Fantine Park novella series, and dozens of short stories that have appeared in web and print publications like *Thuglit*, *Literary Orphans*, and *Great Jones Street*. He also hosts the podcast, *the bastard title*.

HECTOR DUARTE, JR. is a writer and teacher out of Miami, Florida. He was former editor at *The Flash Fiction Offensive*. His work has appeared, among many others, in *Shotgun Honey*, *Spelk Fiction*, *HorrorSleazeTrash*, and *Just to Watch Them Die: Crime Fiction inspired by the songs of Johnny Cash*. His first full-length work, the short story collection *Desperate Times Call*, was published by Shotgun Honey books in September 2018. He loves his wife Samantha and his cat Felina very much.

CARMEN JARAMILLO is a Minnesota-born, half-Panamanian pulp writer. Her stories about people behaving badly have appeared at *The Flash Fiction Offensive*, *Shotgun Honey*, *Switchblade Magazine*, *Noir at the Bar*, the *Writer*

Types podcast, and other venues. She lives in Chicago and is currently working on a novel. Twitter: @jaramilloc2.

JESSICA LAINE writes contemporary crime fiction with a Latin twist. Her work has been published in *Literary Mama*, *Women's Memoir*, and *The Norwegian American*. She is the winner of the 2017 Sisters in Crime Eleanor Taylor Bland award and the 2016 Mystery Writers of America-Midwest Hugh Holton award. Her short story "Lust to Love" was published in the mystery anthology *Murder-A-Go-Go's* by Down & Out Books.

RICHIE NARVAEZ (aka R. Narvaez) was born and raised in Williamsburg, Brooklyn. His literary and crime fiction have been published in *Mississippi Review*, *Murdaland*, *Pilgrimage*, *Indian Country Noir*, *Long Island Noir*, and *Tiny Crimes*. His first collection of short stories, *Roachkiller and Other Stories*, received the 2013 Spinetingler Award for Best Anthology/Short Story Collection and was listed as one of BookRiot's 100 Must-Read Works of Noir. His debut novel *Hipster Death Rattle* was published in 2019.

CHRISTOPHER NOVAS is a Dominican-American writer born and raised in New York. He has recently graduated with an MFA from The New School. This is his first published story.

CYNTHIA (CINA) PELAYO grew up in a haunted house with very superstitious parents. So a lifelong fascination with Gothic literature, romantic horror and the macabre seemed fitting. Pelayo holds a genuine curiosity for superstition, folklore and myth. She holds a Bachelor of Arts in

Journalism from Columbia College, a Master of Science in Integrated Marketing Communication from Roosevelt University, and a Master of Fine Arts in Writing from The School of the Art Institute of Chicago. She is a member of the Horror Writer's Association and is also the Publisher/Gravedigger at Burial Day Books. She wears black most of the time and she stays out of the sun as much as (un)humanly possible. BurialDay.com.

ALEX SEGURA is a novelist and comic book writer. He is the author of the Pete Fernandez Miami Mysteries, which include *Silent City*, *Down the Darkest Street*, and the latest, *Dangerous Ends*. He has also written a number of comic books, including the bestselling and critically acclaimed *Archie Meets Kiss* storyline, the "Occupy Riverdale" story, *Archie Meets Ramones*, and the upcoming *The Archies* one-shot. He lives in New York with his wife and son. He is a Miami native.

DÉSIRÉE ZAMORANO is an award-winning short story writer and the author of the critically acclaimed novel *The Amado Women*. You can find her story "Deep State" in the Anthony Award-winning collection *The Obama Inheritance*. Her essay and short story credits include *Catapult*, *Cultural Weekly*, *Huizache*, and the *Kenyon Review*. She is a frequent contributor to the *LA Review of Books*, with a penchant for the intersection of noir and POC authors. DesireeZamorano.com and @LaDeziree on Twitter.

BOOKS

On the following pages are a few
more great titles from the
Down & Out Books publishing family.

For a complete list of books and to
sign up for our newsletter,
go to DownAndOutBooks.com.

Trouble & Strife
Crime Stories Inspired by Cockney Rhyming Slang
Simon Wood, Editor

Down & Out Books
December 2019
978-1-64396-056-2

Welcome to the world of Cockney rhyming slang, where what is said means something completely different than it sounds. Originally, it was a coded language created by criminals for deceiving undercover police officers during Victorian times. For *Trouble & Strife*, those coded and colorful phrases became the inspiration for eleven killer crime stories.

Edited by Simon Wood with stories by Steve Brewer, Susanna Calkins, Colin Campbell, Angel Luis Colón, Robert Dugoni, Paul Finch, Catriona McPherson, Travis Richardson, Johnny Shaw, Jay Stringer, and Sam Wiebe.

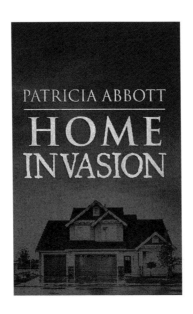

Home Invasion
Patricia Abbott

Down & Out Books
October 2019
978-1-64396-036-4

Home Invasion looks at two members of the Batch family over forty years, and demonstrates the ways in which alcohol, petty crime, poor parenting, and bad choices have had a negative impact on them.

Each story in the book advances their journey by a number of years. *Home Invasion* examines poverty, poor education, crime, sexual identity, parenting and other contemporary issues.

The Hurt Business
Stories by Mike Miner

All Due Respect, an imprint of
Down & Out Books
978-1-948235-75-4

"We are such fragile creatures."

The men, women and children in these stories will all be pushed to the breaking point, some beyond. Heroes, villains and victims. The lives Miner examines are haunted by pain and violence. They are all trying to find redemption. A few will succeed, but at a terrible price. All of them will face the consequences of their bad decisions as pipers are paid and chickens come home to roost. The lessons in these pages are learned the very hard way. Throughout, Miner captures the savage beauty of these dark tales with spare poetic prose.

Chasing China White
Allan Leverone

Shotgun Honey, an imprint of
Down & Out Books
September 2019
978-1-64396-029-6

When heroin junkie Derek Weaver runs up an insurmountable debt with his dealer, he's forced to commit a home invasion to wipe the slate clean.

Things go sideways and Derek soon finds himself a multiple murderer in the middle of a hostage situation.

With seemingly no way out, he may discover the key to redemption lies in facing down long-ignored demons.

Printed in Great
Britain
by Amazon